The HAPPY HOLLISTERS at Sea Gull Beach

A gift of a lighthouse lamp to the Hollister children from their Uncle Russ is found to contain a real emerald. The discovery prompts a visit to Sea Gull Beach to find out where it came from. In a search for a century-old treasure buried with a mystery ship, the Hollisters experience both fun and real excitement. Holly and Sue are caught on a sandbar with an incoming tide and are rescued by their new friend, Rachel. Pete visits the sea bottom and also enters his sea-gull kite in a big kite contest. Clues that eventually lead the Hollisters to treasure include a strange half-house and an old tomb.

The
HAPPY HOLLISTERS
at Sea Gull Beach

BY JERRY WEST

Illustrated by HELEN S. HAMILTON

Publishers • GROSSET & DUNLAP • New York
A FILMWAYS COMPANY

Library of Congress Catalog Card No. 79-88131

ISBN: 0-448-16872-3

Contents

The
HAPPY HOLLISTERS
at Sea Gull Beach

CHAPTER 1

Ship Ahoy!

PETE and Pam Hollister roller skated along the sidewalk as fast as their flying feet would carry them. They wanted to catch the mailman.

"Oh, Mr. Barnes!" Pam called out, her brown eyes dancing with excitement. "Have you a letter for us from Uncle Russ?"

As the gray-haired man smiled and stopped, Pete and Pam skidded to a halt in front of their rambling home.

"I believe there is a letter for the Happy Hollister children," Mr. Barnes said, reaching into his bag. "It's postmarked Sea Gull Beach."

"That's it!" Pete cried gleefully, as he ran his fingers through his blond, crew-cut hair.

As the man handed Pam the letter, the children kicked off their skates and sat down on the lawn.

Pam opened the letter and glanced eagerly at it.

"Uncle Russ says there's a pirate ship at Sea Gull Beach!" she exclaimed.

"A pirate ship?" Pete cried. "Here, let me read it too," he begged.

Pete, the oldest of the five Hollister children, was

"I wish I could see that pirate ship!"

twelve. He was a friendly boy, with frank blue eyes, a broad smile and husky shoulders. His sister, Pam, who was two years younger, had blond hair, which she wore in a fluffy bob. All of her friends in Shoreham liked her because she was kind and generous.

"Oh boy!" Pete said as he read Uncle Russ's letter. "I wish I could see that pirate ship."

The children's favorite uncle, who looked much like their tall, good-looking father, was a newspaper cartoonist. He had gone to Sea Gull Beach to make sketches, and the Hollisters had been looking forward to this letter which he had promised them.

"Read it out loud," Pam urged.

"Okay. Uncle Russ says:

'Last week I came upon a group here who are looking for a pirate ship named the *Mystery*. It was wrecked one hun-

6

dred years ago, and they're sure it must be buried somewhere in this area. How would you like to visit me for a
short vacation and hunt for the treasure ship, too? Ask
mother and dad to bring you.

With love,
Uncle Russ

P.S. Tell your mother I'm sending her a surprise package.'"

"Wouldn't it be great if we could hunt for pirate
treasure?" Pete said as they jumped up. "Say," he
added, "what's that funny mark on the envelope?"

Next to the postmark was a big blue square with a
picture in it of a boy flying a kite. Underneath were
the words:

CHAMPIONSHIP KITE FLYING CONTEST

SEA GULL BEACH

August 17

"That's keen," Pete said. "If we go to see Uncle
Russ, maybe I can enter it."

"Do you suppose girls can, too?" Pam asked.

"I'll write and find out," he answered.

As Pam put the letter into her pocket, seven-year-
old Ricky Hollister came running down the driveway,
pulling a coaster wagon and yelling like an Indian.
Sitting inside the wagon and holding on tightly were
his two younger sisters, Holly, six, and Sue, four.

When Ricky saw Pete and Pam, he swerved toward them. The wagon tilted and the smaller girls
rolled onto the lawn. They picked themselves up,
laughing, and Sue said:

7

Ricky swerved toward them.

"Ricky, you made me lose my hoppergrass."

Puzzled, Ricky stared at his little sister. Then he realized what she meant.

"Don't worry, I'll catch another grasshopper for you," Ricky volunteered.

Ricky was the only one in the Hollister family who had reddish hair. It was usually mussed up, which seemed to go well with his freckles, turned-up nose, blue eyes and pixy smile.

Holly was much like Ricky, except that she had brown eyes and dark hair. It was braided in two pigtails, which hung over her shoulders.

Before Ricky had a chance to take off after another grasshopper, Pam said, "We have a letter from Uncle Russ. He wants us to hunt for a pirate treasure."

"Yikes!" Ricky exclaimed, giving another whoop.

8

Pam read the letter aloud.

"That's neat," Ricky burst out.

Holly skipped up and down. "I've always wanted to be a lady pirate," she said.

"Let's tell Mother about this," Pam proposed.

The five Hollisters ran pell-mell to their lovely home, which was situated on the shore of Pine Lake. Mrs. Hollister, a pretty, young-looking woman with blond hair, was in the living room watering some ivy. Pam said "surprise!" and gave her the letter to read.

"Well, this is an exciting idea," Mrs. Hollister commented, smiling.

"May we go find the pirate ship?" Holly asked.

"It would be a grand trip, wouldn't it," her mother agreed. "We'll have to ask Daddy."

Mr. Hollister was the proprietor of *The Trading Post*, one of Shoreham's most popular stores. It was a combination hardware and sporting goods shop. In one corner were all kinds of toys.

"Daddy's coming home to lunch," Mrs. Hollister said. "We can ask him about the trip then." With that, a faraway look came into her eyes. "I wonder what kind of surprise Uncle Russ is sending me," she added. "I just can't wait to see it."

"Perhaps he painted some sea shells for decorations," Pam guessed. "Uncle Russ is a wonderful painter."

Sue looked up very seriously at her mother. "I wish he'd send us our cousins Jean and Teddy," she said.

"I can just see them coming by mail," Pete

9

chuckled, "with postage stamps pasted all over them!"

Jean and Teddy were the children of Uncle Russ and Aunt Marge. They lived in Crestwood, the town in which the Hollisters used to live.

"I'd love to see your cousins too," Mrs. Hollister said, laughing. Then as she looked out the window, she added, "Here comes Daddy now. We'll ask him if he wants to be a treasure hunter."

Before their father had time to climb out of his station wagon, the children raced up to him. He picked up Sue, tossed her high into the air and caught her. The other children began to talk all at once.

"Can we hunt for a pirate ship?"

"Uncle Russ wants us to."

The children raced up to him.

"Mother thinks it's a good idea."

"When can we go, Daddy?"

Mr. Hollister put Sue down and scratched his head. "Wait a second. What's all this about? One question to a customer."

Pam quickly told him about the letter and asked whether they all could go pirate-ship hunting at Sea Gull Beach.

"That depends," he began.

"On the pirates?" Ricky piped up.

"On business," their father replied.

Mr. Hollister explained that there was so much activity at *The Trading Post* it would be impossible for him to leave the store right now.

"But we might go later," he added, seeing the looks of disappointment on his children's faces.

"Before the seventeenth?" Pete said eagerly, thinking of the kite contest.

"Maybe. But that's only a half promise."

Pete and the others looked relieved, and Pam said, "While we're waiting to go to Sea Gull Beach, let's play pirate."

"That'd be swell," Pete agreed. "We can put on a show in our back yard."

"And sell tickets," Ricky shouted. "Yikes! Let's start it this afternoon."

During lunch the children talked about the pirate play. When they finished eating, all of them rushed into the back yard, which extended from the house to the lake front.

11

He set logs to look like cannon.

Halfway to the dock stood a wooden flagpole. Reaching it, Pete stopped and looked up. "This will be the mast of the pirate ship," he said. "We'll nail rungs on it and a yardarm near the top."

Ricky looked at the lawn. "Let's mark out the deck on the grass with pieces of wood. There's plenty of it alongside the garage."

"What can Holly and I do?" Pam asked.

"We'll need more players," Pete said. "Why don't you make up a play and then get some of our friends to be in it?"

Pam said she would do this, and hurried off with Holly to round up several playmates. While they were gone, Sue watched her brothers prepare the outdoor stage.

Pete nailed rungs up the flagpole and fastened a

12

yardarm securely to the top. Ricky laid pieces of wood on the grass in the shape of a ship's deck. Then he set logs on boxes to look like cannon.

"We're all ready for the attack," he shouted.

"Who are you 'tacking?" Sue asked.

"Sue's right," Pete chuckled. "We must have another boat."

He glanced at their rowboat tied to the dock. "Let's pull her out of the water, Ricky, and put wheels on it. Then we can roll her alongside the pirate ship."

The idea of wheels on anything appealed to Ricky. In the cellar were four old ones which he had recently taken off his coaster wagon. He got them and helped his brother attach the wheels to the lower part of the rowboat.

While the boys were rolling it around, Pam and

"I'm the new captain."

Holly came back, followed by their lovely collie, Zip. The dog began to bark excitedly, thinking this was a good game.

"He's a pirate dog now," Sue giggled.

With Pam and Holly were Jeff and Ann Hunter, Dave Mead and Donna Martin, the Hollister children's best friends.

"Here are the rest of the actors," Pam said gaily. "How about making Dave captain of the pirate ship, and Pete, you be the captain of the American ship that's chasing him."

"Swell," said Dave, a slender, red-cheeked boy about Pete's age. Then he grinned. "I suppose I'll be captured in the end."

"You bet!" said Ricky.

Ten-year-old Ann, who had gray eyes and dark curly hair, was chosen to be a member of the pirate crew, along with her eight-year-old brother Jeff, and Donna, who was seven.

Holly wanted to be a pirate too, and Pam said she might, but added, "The rest of us will be in Pete's crew—and capture you!"

Suddenly another boy came running up the drive. He was a little larger than Pete, with black hair and squinty eyes.

"Hey, what's going on here?" he shouted.

"Oh, that Joey Brill!" Pam whispered to Pete. "He would have to see what we're doing."

Joey was an unfriendly boy who continually annoyed children smaller than himself. He had made

14

lots of trouble for the Hollisters since they had moved to Shoreham.

"We're having a pirate play," Pete said, without explaining further.

"Then I want to be the pirate captain," Joey demanded.

"Dave's already been picked for captain," Pam spoke up.

Joey thrust out his chin. "Oh, yeah? Well, I'm going to change that." He moved toward Dave. "I'm the new captain," he shouted at the boy and gave him a hard shove.

CHAPTER 2

The Old Sailor

DAVE stumbled backward. When he regained his balance, he went for Joey. But before he could hit him, Pam called out:

"Let's not have a fight. You can be in the play, Joey."

"But you can't be the captain of the pirate ship," Pete told him.

"What can I be then?" Joey asked sullenly.

"You can be first mate to Pirate Captain Dave," Pam suggested.

"I don't want to be second to anybody," Joey grumbled.

"All right, then forget about being in the play," Pete replied.

Joey scowled, but finally gave in. "Anyway," he said mysteriously, "I know how I can be a real pirate's first mate."

Before the other actors could ask what he meant, he ran off toward his home.

"There are too many on the pirate side," said Pam. "Jeff, will you go over to the American ship?"

"Sure. Tell us what to do."

16

"He has a wooden leg!"

Pam explained the setup of the play.

"We have to have swords," said Dave.

The boys found some sticks and said these would do.

"When you fight, don't poke anybody with the sticks," Pam warned.

Each child was given a battle station and told what to do and the lines to say. The rehearsal began.

"Avast, me hearties!" cried Ricky, and everyone laughed because this was not in the play.

In the middle of the practice, Joey hobbled up the driveway.

"He has a wooden leg!" Holly cried out.

Joey had cut an old crutch in half and attached it to his knee, after bending the rest of his leg up behind him. As he approached the children, they yelled, "Swell."

Pete added, "That looks good. Just like a real peg-leg pirate, Joey."

Joey proudly took his place on the pirate ship. As the practice went on, Joey shouted orders to his ship-mates, just as if he were the captain instead of the first mate.

"Pipe down!" Dave called to him.

When it came time for the American sailors to board the pirate ship, Ricky jumped onto the enemy boat, waving a wooden sword. Joey flourished his sword at Ricky, and when the little boy ducked, Joey tripped him with his wooden leg. Ricky sprawled headlong on the grassy deck, bumping his head on the "railing" of the pirate ship.

"Ow!" he cried. "That's not fair, Joey."

"I didn't do anything," Joey stormed. "You ran into my wooden leg and fell by yourself."

The two boys might have had a fight but Pam reminded them that the rehearsal must go on.

The children practiced until supper time. Pam declared the show looked pretty good.

"Good enough to sell tickets?" Ricky asked.

"I think so—if we give the money to charity."

"The Crippled Children's Hospital," Ann suggested and the others thought this a fine idea.

After supper, Pam and Holly asked their mother if they might get some old clothes out of the rag bag to make the pirate costumes. Mrs. Hollister said yes,

Pete's crew leaped on to the pirate ship.

there were plenty of colorful odds and ends they might use. She had saved bits of pretty dress material for just such an occasion as this.

"You'll find the bag in the attic next to the old trunk," she said.

While the girls were rummaging through bits of cloth and discarded clothes, Pete and Ricky talked about tickets for the play. Mr. Hollister gave them some old business cards, left over from his store before he had bought it. Ricky brought out a rubber stamp printing set he had received the Christmas before.

"What'll we say on the cards?" he asked.

There was a little discussion, then the words were decided upon. When the cards were finished, they read:

THE HAPPY HOLLISTERS' PIRATE SHOW
FOR THE BENEFIT
OF
THE CRIPPLED CHILDREN'S HOSPITAL
ADMISSION 25¢
FRIDAY NIGHT   7 P.M.

"Hm, they look swell," Pete said, surveying the stack of printed cards. Then he grinned.

"Look at your hand."

Ricky held out his hands. On the back of the left one was printed the lettering of the ticket!

"Oh, gracious!" Mrs. Hollister exclaimed. "That's indelible ink. It'll be hard to wash off."

Ricky laughed and then said, "Pirates had things printed on 'em. I'll show this to everybody and tell 'em to come to our pirate play."

By this time the girls had come from upstairs carrying red, blue, green and yellow material to make the pirates' costumes. There were a couple of old sailor hats too which Pete and Ricky could use.

"We'll make the costumes first thing in the morning," Pam said. "We won't practice any more until tomorrow afternoon."

After breakfast the next day Pam and Holly quickly busied themselves cutting patterns, stitching the material, and sewing on buttons. Sue had a good time running errands.

Pete and Ricky each grabbed a handful of tickets and went from door to door trying to sell them. Mrs. Hunter bought two tickets from Pete and Mrs. Mead took three from Ricky. Then Donna Martin's mother bought two. Finally the boys had asked everyone in their own neighborhood and walked toward the center of town to sell tickets.

"We're doing all right," Pete said. "We only have ten more tickets to sell and that will make thirty altogether. We can't get any more people than that in our back yard."

"That's right," Ricky agreed. "They'd spill over into the lake!"

When the Hollister boys had only six more tickets to sell, they stopped at a small old-fashioned house set back from the street in a grove of cedar trees. As they approached it, Pete said:

"This is really an old house. See that date in the corner: 1825."

"Do you suppose old people live in it?" Ricky asked with a twinkle.

As if in answer to his question, a wrinkled old man in sailor's clothes appeared on the porch. The boys introduced themselves and asked if he would like to buy a ticket.

"A pirate play, eh?" he said, his eyes crinkling. "I'll be glad to buy a ticket, boys."

"Thank you," Pete replied.

The old man continued, "You see, I used to sail the seven seas myself. Come on inside here and I'll show you a few things from my journeys. My name is Sparr."

The boys walked in and gasped. Every corner of

the living room was filled with souvenirs from ships—
big brass lanterns, anchors and chains, old compasses,
and a large foghorn. On the mantel were three ship
models of sailing vessels.

After the boys had examined everything, Ricky
picked up an old compass. He whispered to Pete:

"I wish we could borrow this for the play."

Mr. Sparr overheard him, and offered to lend it to
them. "After all," he said, smiling broadly, "no ship
can steer a course without a compass. You just take
it along. Be sure to bring it back though, won't you?"

The boys thanked him and promised that they
would. Ricky took the compass, and Pete handed
Mr. Sparr a ticket. Then they said good-by and hurried off.

By noontime they had sold all of their tickets and

Pete handed Mr. Sparr a ticket.

went home. Pete handed the seven fifty to his mother who was very pleased at her sons' success. She said she would take the money to the Crippled Children's Hospital as soon as possible.

That afternoon the Hollisters in costume greeted their playmates who came to practice the play again.

"Say, your costumes are neat," Dave said, gazing at them.

Holly had on a tattered pair of shorts, a red bandanna tied around her neck and a black pirate hat with a white skull and bones. Pete and Ricky wore the sailor hats and tight fitting suits. Pam sported a short skirt and a bright blue blouse with a criss-cross belt through which hung her wooden sword. Sue was dressed in a green skirt and yellow blouse with a perky, flat sailor hat. It was her job to fire the cannon.

Ricky showed them the compass and then mounted it on a box next to the ship's make-believe steering wheel.

"That's swell," Dave said, examining it.

The practice lasted an hour and everyone was pleased. Even Joey had played his part well.

After it was over, Pam said, "Don't forget our show is tomorrow night at seven o'clock. Everybody be here at six-thirty, dressed in costume."

The young actors left the yard, and the Hollisters began to clean up. Suddenly Pete looked at the pirate ship.

"The compass is missing!"

The children prepared for the big show.

His brother and sisters gazed in amazement, as Pete ran after their playmates. Catching up to them, he asked each one if he knew what had become of old Mr. Sparr's compass. Nobody did, but Donna reminded Joey Brill he had been playing with it just before they left.

"I didn't take it!" Joey shouted. "You can't blame me!"

Pete went back to the house. He was worried. The compass was such an old one that he might never be able to replace it. Meanwhile, the other children had hunted all around the yard but had not found the compass.

"What'll we do?" Ricky asked.

"I don't know," Pete replied.

But the next morning he went to call on Mr. Sparr. Pete explained to him that the compass had mysteriously disappeared and how bad they all felt about it.

"If I can't find it," Pete said, "I'll look for another one just like it and buy it for you. Will that be all right?"

"That would be fine," said the kind old man. "But I hope you find the lost one."

During the afternoon the Hollister children made preparations for the big show. First they went to all their friends to borrow extra chairs and benches which they placed on the lawn near the lake front. Then they ate an early supper and dressed.

"I'm just a little scared, aren't you, Pam?" Holly asked.

"Yes, I am," Pam admitted. "Oh, I hope everything goes all right."

They watched eagerly for the first people to arrive. Mr. and Mrs. Hunter came early with Jeff and Ann, and soon afterward Dave Mead's parents walked in with Mrs. Martin and Donna.

Pete showed the grownups to seats in the front row. Then as seven o'clock approached, the rest of the audience flocked into the Hollisters' back yard.

"Oh, how pretty the setting is!" one woman remarked. "It's so real, and those children do look like pirates."

As it came time for the show to start, Pete climbed the rungs of the flagpole and tied a stout rope to the yardarm. This was going to be part of Holly's act.

Pam looked for the enemy ship.

Promptly at seven Pete stood before the audience and announced:

"Ladies and gentlemen, this is a pirate play in two acts. In the first act, the pirates drive off the American sailors. In the second act, the American boat attacks and captures the pirates. We hope you enjoy it."

As they clapped, he took his place in the boat on wheels and the show started. How well everybody played his part! Even Joey Brill with his loud voice acted just like a bad pirate.

Ricky pushed the rowboat close to the pirate ship with the *boom boom* of the cannon, played on a record. After a clash of wooden swords, the good sailors were driven back. The audience cheered as the first act came to a close.

The second part opened with Pam putting her

hand to her forehead and scanning the horizon for the enemy ship. Sue "fired" the wooden cannon again and again and the ship on wheels came nearer to the pirates' boat. When they touched, Pete looked up at the pirates' red and black flag, flying from the top of the pole and cried out:

"Strike down your flag, pirates, or we shall sink your ship!"

"Ho ho—let's see you try." Captain Dave, the pirate, whipped out his sword.

Pete gave the word to his crew, and they leaped onto the pirate ship. Holly climbed up the mast, with Ricky scrambling after her.

"I'll catch you!" he shouted. "Halt! Avast!"

Holly, nimble as a monkey, scooted up to the yard-arm. Then she grabbed hold of the rope and started to slide down. When she was halfway to the ground, Joey Brill grabbed hold of the rope and began to jiggle it.

"Stop that!" Holly cried.

"You shouldn't fight against one of your own crew!" Dave Mead cried out.

But by now it was too late. The rope was securely tangled around Holly's left leg. Her hands lost their grip, and she dangled upside down in midair, swinging by one ankle!

CHAPTER 3

The Surprise Package

"GRAB her! Don't let her fall!" Mrs. Mead cried out.

Several other spectators called out in alarm when they saw Holly dangling from the rope.

"Oh, that poor child!" said Mrs. Martin.

Mr. Hollister had dashed to the deck of the pirate ship and stood beneath his daughter in case she should fall. Pete and Ricky meanwhile had raced into the Hollister garage and now returned with a step ladder. They quickly set it against the pole and Pete climbed up.

By standing on top of the ladder, he could just reach his sister's ankle. As the audience cheered, Pete freed Holly and lifted her to the ladder. Then they both scrambled down the rungs. The ladder was carried back to the garage. Then Pete went over to Joey.

"Don't try anything like that again," he warned him, "or there'll be trouble! If Holly had fallen, she would have hurt herself badly."

Joey grumbled that he had not meant to harm her. Then Pete turned to the audience and announced:

"The play will continue!"

With a *whack* and a *thwack* of wooden swords, the battle was on again. Pam dropped her sword, and Dave Mead shouted:

"You're my prisoner!" He quickly tied her to the mast of the pirate ship.

With one of their number captured, the good sailors decided to retreat for a moment to the boat on wheels and plan what they should do next.

Meanwhile the pirate captain shouted, "Our prisoner must be blindfolded and walk the plank!"

"Oh," sighed a little girl in the front row, "they wouldn't do that to a girl!"

Sue overheard the remark and turned to the child, her perky little pirate hat tilting on the side of her head.

"Don't worry," Sue said. "This is only make-believe."

Everybody laughed, and the worried little girl in the audience felt better. Meanwhile, the pirate captain had placed a board on the grass, extending it out over the prow of the pirate ship's deck. Pam's hands were bound behind her and she was blindfolded. Then Dave ordered:

"Now walk out to the end of the plank and jump off!"

"They can't do this to a U.S. sailor!" Pete shouted. "Come on, men! We'll attack again!"

The rowboat on wheels was pushed alongside the

pirate ship again and Pete rallied his crew by shouting:

"We must save Pam!"

What a scuffle followed on the deck of the pirate ship! Pete rushed over to his sister and untied her wrists. Then he gave her a new sword and the make-believe battle went on.

One by one, the pirates were disarmed and their wrists were tied behind them. Finally Joey Brill was the only pirate left.

"Surrender now!" Ricky cried out.

"I will not!" Joey retorted.

Suddenly Pam whispered, "Joey, this is the way we planned to do it. All the pirates have to give up. That's the way the play ends."

"Walk the plank and jump off!"

"I don't care how the play is supposed to end!" Joey shouted defiantly.

He continued to fight hard, swinging his sword with such force that it stung the hands of the other children.

"This is only a make-believe fight," Pete told him. "It's time to give up. The play should be over."

Gradually the audience sensed that all was not going well with the pirate play. Even though Joey was supposed to surrender, he did not want to do as directed.

"I won't give up to any girl," he shouted.

"They're supposed to be sailors," Holly told him, dodging his sword. By this time Joey was hitting pirates as well as American sailors.

Suddenly Pete saw an opportunity to knock the sword out of Joey's hand. With a quick thrust he sent it flying to the deck of the pirate ship.

"Now you're my prisoner!" Pete exclaimed.

"That's what you think!" Joey said rudely.

He swung his fist and hit Pete on the shoulder. Pete hit him back on the chin. The boys grappled with each other and fell to the deck of the pirate ship, rolling over and over.

"Stop, stop!" Pam shouted, trying to pull the fighting boys apart.

Dave Mead helped her, and as the boys were separated, Holly quickly tied a rope around Joey's wrists.

"Now he's captured," she announced proudly.

31

"Ladies and gentlemen, the play is over!"

As Joey squirmed and kicked, Pete faced the audience. "Ladies and gentlemen," he panted, out of breath, "the pirate play is over. All the pirates have been captured and the high seas are once more free for American vessels."

"Hurrah!" shouted Mr. Sparr with a grin, as the audience applauded.

"That was wonderful," Mrs. Mead said. "It's too bad Joey had to start a fight when everything was going so nicely."

Several spectators complimented the children and praised them for helping the Crippled Children's Hospital.

Shortly after breakfast the next day they saw an expressman pull up in front of the Hollister home.

He hopped out with a box under his arm and walked to the front door.

"Mrs. Hollister?" he inquired, as she opened the screen door.

"That's right."

"A package for you. Handle it gently because it's marked fragile."

When the man left, Mrs. Hollister looked at the postmark and exclaimed, "This is the surprise from Uncle Russ!"

By this time all the Hollister children had gathered around their mother, eager to see what was inside of the box.

"Don't open it until we all have a guess," Pam suggested, giggling.

"All right," Mrs. Hollister agreed. "What do you think it is?"

Pete said that it might be a sailing ship built inside a bottle. Pam thought it was a set of dishes with the name Sea Gull Beach painted on them. Ricky imagined it to be sea shells, and Holly a pirate doll. Sue hoped it would be candy.

"Well, now we'll see who was right," Mrs. Hollister said, placing the package on the table.

She opened the box carefully so as not to break its contents and felt inside the shavings. Finally she pulled out something wrapped in tissue paper.

"Oh, it's a lighthouse!" she cried.

The beautiful ornament was made of colorful clay and stood about a foot high.

"Oh, it's a lighthouse!"

Pete looked at it closely. "It has a light in the tower, Mother. And here's a cord. Let's plug it in and see how it works."

He inserted the plug in a wall socket and turned the lamp on. It beamed faintly in the daylight.

"How pretty!" said Mrs. Hollister. "This will be nice in the upstairs hall. We'll leave it on all night. Turn it off, Pete."

For the time being, Mrs. Hollister set the lighthouse lamp on the living room mantel.

A moment later the children's attention was drawn to the front yard where the mailman was coming up the front walk. Pete ran out to meet him.

"A letter for you," Mr. Barnes said, handing a white envelope to the boy.

"From Sea Gull Beach!" Pete exclaimed with a

grin. "About the kite flying contest. I wrote them a couple of days ago."

He sat down on the front steps, tore open the envelope and read the letter. As he finished, his brother and sisters came outside.

"What's it say?" Ricky asked.

The kite flying contest, Pete told them, was to be held on the seventeenth and was open both to boys and girls, ten years and older.

"Good!" Pam cried.

There would be several prizes—one for the largest kite, another for the most unusual, and a third for the special box kite division.

"Oh, I hope we can go to Sea Gull Beach and get into this contest," Pete said.

"It's real windy along the shore, isn't it?" Ricky piped up. "I'll bet a kite could fly awful high there."

Holly wanted to fly a kite right away that day. Pete thought there was not enough wind, but the two tried it anyway with two old kites they had used the year before. When it was time for lunch, Ricky tied them to a tree. He had no sooner done this than a strong gust of wind began to tug at the cords.

"We'll lose 'em!" cried Holly.

The two children quickly pulled the kites down and took them in the house.

Mr. Hollister did not come home to lunch. When he arrived in the evening, his wife showed him the attractive lamp lighthouse which Uncle Russ had sent her.

"That's fine," he said. "Where are you going to put it?"

"In the second floor hall," she replied.

"Let's take it up now," Pam suggested.

Pete carried the light upstairs, set it on the table and inserted the plug in a nearby socket. Immediately the bright light shone in the top of the lighthouse. Then to everyone's amazement, it began to blink off and on.

"It's just like a real house light," Ricky announced.

They all laughed, and Mrs. Hollister said, "Well, it is a house light and a lighthouse both."

At this moment Zip, who had been downstairs eating his supper, raced up to see what the family was doing. When he saw the blinking lighthouse, he began to bark. Then, trying to get a closer view, the collie jumped onto a chair alongside the table and sniffed at it.

"It doesn't have any smell," Sue told him.

"And you're too big for the chair," Pam said. "Get down, Zip!"

The collie jumped down obediently and walked around the children who were admiring the blinking novelty. But Zip had never seen anything like this before. Even the squirrels which scampered among the trees on the Hollisters' lawn did not intrigue him as much as this strange lamp did.

The dog nudged his mistress with his cool nose as if to say he wanted a closer look, and before Pam could restrain him he jumped into the chair again.

The light fascinated the dog.

"Please! Down Zip," she coaxed.

But the light fascinated the dog. As the others moved away, he stood still, wagging his tail. Suddenly he gave a couple of extra hard wags, and his tail hit the lighthouse. It teetered on the edge of the table.

"Catch it quick!" shouted Holly, who was still watching the dog.

But everything had happened so fast that nobody was able to reach the lighthouse in time. With a crash, it hit the floor!

CHAPTER 4

The Lamp's Secret

WHEN the lighthouse lamp hit the floor, it cracked in half.

"Oh!" Holly cried out. "You naughty dog!"

As Pete bent over to pick up the lamp, Sue started to cry.

"Our beautiful lighthouse is ruined!" she sobbed.

Zip stopped wagging his tail and hung his head.

"It wasn't exactly your fault, old boy," Pam said, patting him. "Your tail wags too hard, that's all."

Mrs. Hollister did not know what to say. Uncle Russ had sent them such a lovely gift, and now it was broken before even being used.

"Don't worry, Mother," Pete consoled her. "I think I can mend the lamp. Dad, you know that new kind of cement *The Trading Post* sells. I'll experiment with it."

"All right, dear," said his mother. "But we'll wait till morning."

"Before you apply the cement, Pete, be sure to roughen up both the surfaces so that the cement will get a firm grip," his father advised.

When Pete awakened the next day, he hopped out

"Our lighthouse is ruined!"

of bed and dressed quickly. His brother and sisters were still sleeping when he tiptoed downstairs. The boy found his mother and father seated at the breakfast table.

"Good morning, Mother and Dad," Pete said.

"Goodness, you're up early," his mother replied, kissing him.

"I thought I'd ride down to *The Trading Post* with Dad and get that cement," Pete said.

He ate with his parents, then drove off with his father. By the time Pete returned with the cement, the other children were halfway through breakfast. Pete explained where he had been, then went to the kitchen.

Presently Mrs. Hollister brought in a dish of soft-boiled eggs and set them on the table. A mischievous look came into Ricky's eyes. After he had cracked an egg and scooped it out into his dish, he slid out of his chair and followed Pete into the kitchen.

"Hey, if that mending cement's any good, how about putting this shell together?" he whispered.

Pete grinned. "Think I can't do it, eh?"

"If you can, I'll play a trick," Ricky said and returned to the table.

He had just finished eating when Pete returned and slipped the mended egg into his brother's hand. When no one was looking, Ricky replaced it in the bowl.

"It sure looks as if it had never been cracked," he thought. Aloud he said, "Holly, there's one egg left. Don't you want it?"

"Oh, you take it," she said.

"I don't want any more egg. Pam, why don't you eat it?"

"No thanks."

Poor Ricky! How was he going to make his joke work? He couldn't ask Sue because she never opened her own eggs.

Mrs. Hollister, who was busy arranging some cut flowers in a bowl, suggested that the boy take it.

Ricky was stumped for a minute. Then he had an idea. "Will you please crack it for me?" he asked.

"Why, Ricky, you're big enough to do that," his mother replied.

"Oh, the egg tastes better when you crack it, Mother," he teased her.

Nothing dropped out!

Mrs. Hollister put down the flowers and went to the table. She reached over and took the egg. Then she cracked it on the side of Ricky's dish and held it up.

Nothing dropped out!

"Why, what—" Mrs. Hollister exclaimed, as Holly, Pam and Sue stared in bewilderment.

Pete and Ricky laughed hard. "Just advertising a good cement," Pete said.

When the other children saw that it was a joke, they all started to laugh and Mrs. Hollister said:

"You boys! You are always up to something. Pete, if you can mend the lamp as well as you did that egg, it will be as good as new."

Pete went back to the cellar, with Ricky following

him. The younger boy watched as his brother took the sharp end of a file and roughened the edges of the broken surfaces by making crisscross marks on the pottery. All at once he exclaimed:

"Hey, Ricky, look! What's this?"

Something green was sticking out of the clay.

"Chip it out," Ricky said excitedly.

Pete carefully dug around the green object and a moment later it fell into his hand. It was about the size of a small pea.

"Say," he cried, "it looks like an emerald!"

"An emerald? That's worth a lot of money!"

"It sure is."

Pete got a rag and wiped the stone. The more he polished it, the brighter it became. Excitedly the two boys rushed upstairs and showed it to Mrs. Hollister.

"It does look genuine," she said. "I think you'd better check on this with Mr. Peters, the jeweler, downtown."

"I'll go with you," Pam offered. "I want to look at something in his store, anyway."

Mrs. Hollister suggested that Ricky stay at home and put the wheels back on his coaster wagon. So Pete and Pam set off without him.

"Well, the Happy Hollisters," said Mr. Peters pleasantly as Pete and Pam came into his shop. "What can I do for you today?"

Pete told him about the green stone they had found and handed it to the jeweler, who peered at it through a magnifying glass.

"Hm," he said, "this is the real thing, all right."

Pushing his spectacles up to his forehead, he looked at Pete and Pam. "This emerald is worth five hundred dollars."

The children gasped. "Five hundred dollars!"

Pete, still hardly believing his ears, held out his hand for the emerald, but the jeweler said, "Something as valuable as this should be carried in a box."

He took down several small boxes.

"Here, I guess this is about the right size," he remarked, opening one and placing the stone on a piece of cotton inside. Then he closed the lid and handed the box to Pam, smiling.

"Be sure to go right home and give it to your mother," he advised.

"Hm, this is the real thing!"

Pam paused though to look at a tray of charm bracelets. She put down the box to try one on.

"Oh, let's go," Pete urged, so they started for home. Reaching the house they ran excitedly to their mother. "It's an emerald. A real gem!" Pam exclaimed.

She handed the box to Mrs. Hollister, who removed the lid. A strange look came over her face.

"Why—why there's nothing in the box, Pam," she said. "Is this another trick?"

Pete and Pam looked alarmed. There was nothing in the box but a fluffy white piece of cotton.

"It's not a trick," Pam wailed. "The stone was in here."

"Then you must have lost it on the way home," Mrs. Hollister said.

"I don't see how we could have, Mother," Pete remarked. "Pam had it in her hand all the time, and we didn't open the box once."

"Nevertheless it's gone," Mrs. Hollister said. "Start from our front door and retrace every step you took."

The other children heard the commotion and said they would help search. Several of their friends joined in the hunt also.

After a while Sue sighed wearily. "This is harder than hunting for Easter eggs," she said.

The searchers covered every inch of ground Pete and Pam had taken but the emerald was not found.

"Maybe somebody picked it up," Holly said as they neared the jewelry shop.

When Mr. Peters saw them peering intently at the sidewalk, he stepped out of his door and said, "What's going on? Did you lose something?"

"We can't find the lovely emerald," Pam said with a woebegone look. She explained to the jeweler how she had arrived home with an empty box.

All at once Mr. Peters' eyes lit up. "Follow me," he said.

The man turned on his heel and went to the counter of his store. Two other little white boxes were lying there. He picked one up and opened it. There on the cotton lay the beautiful gem!

"Pam, you picked up the wrong box after you looked at the bracelets," he smiled.

The girl was so relieved that she nearly burst into tears. She raced all the way home with the box to show Mrs. Hollister the emerald.

"I'm certainly glad you found it," she said. "And isn't it beautiful!"

It took Pete the rest of the morning to mend the broken lamp but he made a very good job of it.

"That's splendid," his mother said.

"Maybe we ought to put the lamp in *The Trading Post* window to advertise the cement," Pete chuckled.

A little while later Mr. Hollister drove home to lunch, and Pam told him about the wonderful gem.

"Don't you think we'd better call up Uncle Russ and ask him who made the lamp?" she said. "If that's the person who lost the emerald, he'll be glad to get it back."

"You're right. Put the call in," her father said, "but let Mother do the talking."

Pam went immediately to the telephone and a few minutes later was connected with her uncle at Sea Gull Beach. Mrs. Hollister took the instrument and thanked her brother-in-law for the lamp. Then she explained how it had been broken, and Pete had found the emerald inside.

"That's amazing," Uncle Russ said. "An elderly woman who lives here made that lighthouse. Her name is Mrs. Alden, but everybody up here calls her Grandma Alden. She'll be excited to hear about this. But say, wouldn't it be a good idea for all of you to come up? Bring the gem and tell her about it."

He added that Aunt Marge and Teddy and Jean

Pete packed the kite material.

would join him soon. It would be fun for all the children to be together.

"Let me talk to John, will you please?" Uncle Russ said.

Mrs. Hollister gave the phone to her husband. Presently a smile came over his face.

"All right, Russ. I guess you win. I'll arrange for all of us to come in a few days. Good-by."

When the children heard this, they began to whoop and jump around. They were going to Sea Gull Beach to hunt for pirate treasure!

"Do you think you can be ready to leave in two days?" Mr. Hollister asked his wife.

"I'm sure we can do it, John."

"Oh boy, I'll be able to fly a kite in the meet!" Pete exclaimed. "Daddy, may I earn some kite material by helping you at *The Trading Post*?"

"Sure thing. Come down with me after lunch."

Pete helped his father for more than a day, and in return got kite sticks, paper, and lots of string and glue, which he packed into his suitcase.

White Nose, the Hollisters' cat, and her five kittens were to be left with Jeff and Ann Hunter. It was decided that Zip would go on the trip with the family.

Finally the time arrived for the Happy Hollisters to leave. The station wagon was packed, and everyone took his place. The children's friends gathered in the driveway, and as the car pulled out, they all shouted:

"Have a good time!"

"Giddap!"

"Win the kite contest, Pete!"

"Find the pirate treasure!"

"Good-by! Good-by!"

As Mr. Hollister drove along, he said to his wife, "I'm glad we got an early start today. We'll be able to make this trip in about a day and a half."

"Where are we going to stay tonight?" Sue asked.

"Oh, that's a surprise," he laughed.

The children became so busy talking about the adventures they might have at Sea Gull Beach that the morning passed very quickly. Finally it was time to stop for lunch. Sue spied a roadside stand which had a pony corral alongside it.

"Please let's stop and have lunch here," she said, "so I can have a pony ride."

"Oh yes, let's," Ricky begged.

48

Her father pulled into the parking lot, and they walked through a gate to a corral. Only one pony was not busy, so Sue had the first turn. The owner lifted her onto one of the cute little animals. Sue held onto the reins and said:

"Giddap!"

She started around the track. How proud and straight Sue carried herself on the pony's back!

On the second time around the corral, the pony suddenly headed for a little gate on the far side. Somebody had left it ajar about two inches. The animal pushed the gate open with his nose and trotted out of the corral.

"Go back!" Sue told him.

But the pony, once he was free, set off at a fast clip. Sue screamed, trying to hold on tightly as the pony jogged along.

He headed straight down the road with the rest of the Hollisters in pursuit.

CHAPTER 5

A Puppy Rescue

"Help! Help!" Sue cried out as she clung to the run-away pony.

Ricky was closest to the gate through which the pony had escaped. He grabbed a long piece of rope that was lying across one of the corral poles and gave chase.

As he ran, the boy made a noose in the rope. When the pony turned into a field and started back, Ricky swung the lariat around and around over his head. Then he threw it.

"Hold tight!" he yelled to Sue.

The little girl dug her fingers in as the lariat landed squarely over the pony's head. Ricky pulled hard, and the animal stopped. Then the frisky pony turned around and came back toward the boy. By this time the rest of the Hollisters had caught up to them.

"Oh, you saved Sue's life," Mrs. Hollister said, as she hugged first her son, then her daughter.

"That was quick thinking, Ricky," his father praised him.

Ricky proudly led the pony back to the corral, where he removed the lariat from its neck. The pony's owner also thanked the boy and apologized for the animal's actions.

"I'm so glad the little girl is all right," he said. "Here's another pony that's too old to try any tricks. You can have all the rides you want on him."

Ricky mounted this pony and rode him around the track several times. Then each of the other children took a turn.

"I think we had better eat now," Mr. Hollister said, glancing at his wrist watch.

He led the way to the attractive luncheonette with stools arranged in a line in front of a sparkling clean counter. After everybody had eaten hamburgers and drunk two glasses of milk, Pam asked for some food for Zip.

She hurried to the car with it and let Zip exercise for a while. Then she fed him and the Hollisters set off again toward Sea Gull Beach.

Toward evening Mr. Hollister stopped again, this time in front of a quaint guest house.

"I hope we can find rooms here," he said.

From the rear came a howling sound. At once the children went to investigate.

"A puppy!" Holly cried. "And he's stuck!"

A wire-haired terrier was caught under the fence of his play yard, as he tried to scratch his way to freedom.

"I'll rescue you," Holly said kindly.

She bent down and eased the puppy out. While she held the frightened little dog in her arms, Pete

"I'll rescue you," Holly said.

filled in the hole, which the puppy had made, with loose dirt and stomped it down.

At this moment Mr. and Mrs. Hollister appeared with a plump, smiling woman. They rushed over to see what had happened.

"Oh, thank you for saving Topsy," the woman said, after hearing the story. "She might have hurt herself. I'll put her in the cellar."

"Oh please let us play with her," Holly begged.

"All right."

Mr. Hollister introduced the woman as Mrs. Worth, the aunt of a friend of his.

"I'm so sorry you didn't make a reservation, Mr. Hollister," Mrs. Worth said. "I have only two small rooms left, and I guess you need more than that."

"Yes, we do," Mrs. Hollister sighed. "Can you tell us where we might find rooms?"

Mrs. Worth said there was not another guest house for miles. But why didn't they have supper with her before setting out again? They accepted and sat down on the porch to wait.

Topsy had the time of her life frisking about with the children until they were called to supper. When they had finished eating, Mrs. Hollister said, rising:

"I hope we'll find a place to sleep before it gets too dark."

Mrs. Worth twisted her hands nervously. "I dislike turning anyone away, especially such nice people as you are. And your children helped Topsy, too. I have a plan," she said. "If you'll let two of your girls sleep in a spare bed in my room, there'll be places for all of you."

"I'd like to sleep in your room," Holly spoke up.

"I would too," said Pam.

"That's very satisfactory," Mrs. Hollister smiled in relief. "And how about Sue?"

"If she won't mind a crib, I'll get one from the attic."

"I don't want to be a baby again," Sue objected.

"You won't mind this crib," Mrs. Worth laughed and asked Pete and Ricky to help her bring it downstairs.

Sue trotted after them. When she saw the bed she fell in love with it. It looked just like a big four poster with a canopy top, only it had side rails on it.

"I wish I could keep it," the little girl said, when the crib was placed in her parents' room.

The little girl wanted to go to bed at once!

Before Pam said good night, she gave Zip some supper and ran around the yard with him for fifteen minutes. Then she put a blanket on the floor of the station wagon so the dog could sleep there comfortably for the night.

The Hollister children were so tired from their long ride, they went to sleep immediately. By nine the next morning, however, the whole family, refreshed, was on its way toward Sea Gull Beach. As they drove along, the children became more and more excited.

"We're getting nearer and nearer the pirate ship," Ricky cried.

"See how flat the countryside is," Pam said.

"That's because we're nearing the seashore," her mother explained.

It was not long before they were driving through sandy country in which scrubby pine trees grew on either side of the road. When they came to a sign with an arrow pointing to Sea Gull Beach, the children cried out with glee.

"It won't be long now," Holly said, bouncing in the seat.

"Hm, smell that wonderful salt air!" Mrs. Hollister remarked.

Then suddenly ahead of them lay the beautiful blue-green ocean. Far out on the horizon, they could see the smokestacks of a large ship.

"Is it going to Spain, do you suppose?" asked Ricky who was studying about Spain in school.

"No, it's just a coastwise steamer," Mr. Hollister replied.

The road paralleled the ocean for many miles. As they drove along, they saw small fishing boats with sails and a few motorboats. There were several airplanes, too, which skimmed low over the water.

A quarter of a mile farther on was a big sign at the side of the road. It read:

WELCOME TO SEA GULL BEACH

Mr. Hollister stopped the car and pulled a piece of paper from his pocket. On it were directions to Uncle Russ's house. Mr. Hollister followed the instructions carefully and presently he came to a gray-

"Sea Gull Beach!" they cried out with glee.

shingled rambling house just back of a wide beach. He tooted his horn three times and a tall, handsome man appeared at the front door of the house.

"Uncle Russ! Hello, Uncle Russ!" the Hollisters shouted.

The children scrambled from the car as fast as they could and bounded up to him. Zip, too, was happy to be there. He ran around in circles and began sniffing the sand.

After Uncle Russ had greeted everyone, he picked up little Sue.

"You've grown two inches since I saw you," he laughed.

"Uncle Russ," she begged, "let's do one of our tricks."

"Sure thing." He lifted Sue to his shoulders.

Then, pitching his head forward, he gave her a double flip flop before landing her on the ground. Smoothing out his rumpled hair, he said to his brother:

"John, what do you think of this place?"

"Very fine."

"There's enough room in it for a regiment," Russ went on, "but we'll need it when my family arrives."

The house was built in the shape of an L. In the corner of the L was a lovely lawn edged with flowers, and many comfortable chairs were scattered about.

"I know we'll enjoy it," Mrs. Hollister said.

"And we're going to find the pirate treasure!" Ricky exclaimed.

Pete, Pam and Holly ran to the beach.

"Divers are working on this already, but they haven't found anything yet," Uncle Russ said.

"Oh goody!" Holly shouted and danced about. "Maybe we'll find the treasure first!"

The Hollister boys and their father quickly unpacked the station wagon and put the suitcases in the rooms which their uncle designated. When this was done, and the clothes hung up, Pete, Pam and Holly ran down to the beach.

"Aren't those sea gulls lovely?" Pam exclaimed, watching the graceful birds swooping down to catch fish from the sea.

"There must be a million of 'em," Holly said. Throwing out her arms like wings she began to race around imitating them.

Pam hurried down to the water's edge, but had to scramble back quickly as a large wave broke on the shore near her toes and sent foaming suds racing along the sand.

"Let's take off our shoes," Pete suggested.

The children did this, tucking them under their arms and walking through the water. A little farther along and about thirty feet back from where the waves broke, steep hills of sand rose up from the beach.

"These dunes are really high," Pam said. "Aren't they pretty?"

The slopes of the dunes were streaked with color from brown to a deep red.

After they had walked down the beach a way, the children noticed a girl about Pam's age in a bathing suit seated on top of one of the dunes. Her elbows touched her knees and her chin was cupped in her hands. She was looking pensively across the water.

"Let's speak to her," Holly suggested.

When the children drew nearer, the girl glanced down and saw them. They waved, and she waved back.

"Hello," she said, smiling. "You've just come, haven't you?"

"Yes," said Holly, "but how did you know?"

"You haven't any tan," the girl giggled. "Are you brother and sisters?"

Pam introduced herself, Holly and Pete. Then the girl said:

"My name is Rachel Snow. I'm spending the summer with my grandmother."

Rachel slid down the dune.

Pam noticed immediately what a pretty girl Rachel was. She had auburn hair, wide brown eyes and a dimple in her right cheek when she smiled. Rachel slid down the dune to where they were standing.

"We've come to visit our uncle and find the pirate treasure," Holly spoke up.

"People have been trying to find that treasure for a long time," Rachel said. "Some new divers have a camp down the beach and a barge out on the ocean. But they can't find the treasure, either."

"What were you doing on top of the dune?" Pam asked.

Rachel smiled. "I was looking across **to Spain**," she said.

Rachel picked up a stick and drew a map in the sand showing the Hollisters that if they were to sail due East they would come to the southern part of Spain.

As Rachel was explaining this, Holly wandered off to the foot of a giant dune, where she had spotted a large sea shell. As Pete glanced in her direction, he suddenly cried out in alarm.

Near the top of the dune a log had started to roll down the sandy slope. It kicked up puffs of sand as it tumbled straight toward Holly, who did not see it!

CHAPTER 6

A Mean Crab

"HOLLY! Get out of the way!" Pete shouted, as he saw the log hurtling down the sand dune toward his sister.

But Holly did not understand what he was talking about, so Pete raced to her side and flung himself toward her. He pushed Holly onto the sand just as the log rolled past them. It had missed the girl by inches.

"Oh!" she gasped, sitting up. "How lucky for me you looked over here, Pete!" and she hugged her big brother thankfully.

By this time Rachel and Pam had run over to them. As they all glanced up the steep side of the dune from where the log had come, Pete declared, "That just didn't start down by itself."

"You mean—" Pam began, her eyes growing wide.

"Yes, somebody pushed it off the top of the dune," her brother finished.

"Let's find out who did it," Rachel suggested.

The children had to dig in with their hands as well as their feet to climb the dune. Finally they reached the grassy top and looked about them. No one was in sight.

Suddenly Pam shouted, "I see someone! Over there!"

She pointed and the children saw a boy's figure in the distance between the scrub pines that fringed the beach. He was running as fast as he could and soon disappeared.

"I'm sure I know who that is," Rachel said. "Homer Ruffly."

"Does he live around here?" asked Pete.

"Not exactly," Rachel answered. She explained that Homer was the son of the head of the treasure-hunting party.

"He's about thirteen years old, and can be very mean," Rachel went on. "Just the other day he ducked some small children in the waves."

The Hollisters asked about Mr. Ruffly's party, and Rachel said the treasure hunters sent their diver down

Suddenly Pam shouted, "I see someone!"

from the barge every day looking for the old pirate ship, the *Mystery*.

"Mr. Ruffly isn't liked any better than his son," Rachel said, "because he's always bragging about how he's going to find the treasure before any of the local people do."

"We'll have to watch out for Homer and his father," Pam said.

As the three Hollister children and their new-found friend walked back up the beach, Pam asked Rachel if she knew where Mrs. Alden lived.

"Why," replied the girl in a surprised voice, "I'm staying with her for the summer."

"You are?" It was Pam's turn to be surprised. "Then—she's your grandmother!"

"Yes," Rachel replied, smiling.

On hearing this, Holly was the first to burst out, "Oh! We have a wonderful treasure for her!"

As Rachel looked at Holly, astonished, the other children nodded vigorously. Pete then explained why they must see Grandma Alden at once. When he had told about finding the emerald, Rachel's eyes glowed with delight.

"Follow me," she urged. "We'll go to Grandma's right now!"

The children quickly put their shoes back on, and ran after Rachel along a path that wound through a valley in the dunes.

Soon they were in the center of the small town of Sea Gull Beach. It was a quaint place, with little white cottages and neat yards. Presently they came to a narrow street.

Rachel turned in and stopped before a simple, but trim, cottage. As the children went up the walk, a sweet-faced woman, with gray hair, came to the door.

"Why, Rachel," she said, looking very pleased. "I see you've found some new friends."

"Indeed I have," Rachel replied and introduced the Hollisters to Mrs. Alden.

"You may call me Grandma," the woman said.

She invited them into her living room. When they had sat down in the big, old-fashioned chairs, Rachel announced:

"Grandma, my friends have some exciting news for you."

"Really? I should love to hear what it is."

Holly started telling about the lighthouse lamp their mother had received from Uncle Russ.

"And when it broke," Pam put in, "we found a treasure in it."

At this point, Pete continued, "Yes, there was a real emerald in the clay, and the jeweler says it's worth about five hundred dollars."

Grandma Alden's eyes sparkled with amazement and pleasure as she listened, but now she looked a little quizzical.

"Well, my dears," said the old lady, "the emerald must have been in the clay which I used to make the lighthouse. I suppose you might say it belongs to me although I really didn't lose it."

When Pete and the other Hollisters insisted that she should have the gem, Grandma Alden arose and said, "I'd be very happy to talk this over with your mother. Why don't you bring her here after lunch?"

The children agreed to do this. Saying good-by to Mrs. Alden, they started back. Rachel walked with her new friends to the beach. She said she would go with them part of the way to Uncle Russ's house.

As they strolled along the sand, the Hollisters poked at the strange objects cast up by the waves.

"What is this funny thing with the long tail?" Holly asked Rachel.

"That's the shell of a horseshoe crab," the girl replied, taking a stick and turning it over.

Pete picked up a starfish, and Pam found several beautiful small shells. Rachel told her that they were shells of baby scallops and that many people painted them as souvenirs.

"What are those high rocks up ahead there, Rachel?" Holly asked, pointing to a line of glistening boulders which extended far out into the waves.

"That's called a jetty," Rachel explained. "It keeps the sea from washing the shore away."

The Hollister children raced ahead to examine the jetty. The huge rocks were piled about five feet high, and, as the waves broke against them, they sent up tall plumes of spray. The surface of the rocks was slippery and covered with moss.

"Be careful when you climb them," Rachel warned

65

Holly scrambled to the top.

Holly, who was already scrambling to the top of the jetty.

"I will," Holly replied. She shaded her eyes from the sun and looked up and down the beach. "Somebody's running toward us. Oh, it's Ricky."

In a couple of minutes the freckle-nosed boy raced up to them. After Pam introduced him to Rachel, Ricky said:

"I want to get something alive to take home."

"How about a crab for a pet?" Pam teased.

"N-no," her brother said.

"Would you like some periwinkles?" Rachel suggested.

"What are they?"

"I'll show you," said Rachel and led him to the foot of the jetty. She pointed to little round, black objects clustered on the side of one of the rocks.

"They're holding onto the rocks by one foot," Ricky cried, bending so close his nose almost touched the tiny shelled creatures.

"That's the only foot it has," Rachel laughed.

"I'm going to take some of these home," Ricky announced, looking around for a container.

Not far away, on the beach, was a red and blue jar which somebody apparently had left there after a picnic. Ricky half filled it with sea water, then he plucked ten periwinkles from the rock and dropped them into the jar.

"Put a little stone in, too," Rachel advised, "so the periwinkles will have something to hold on to."

Ricky found three large pebbles and added them to the jar. At this moment, Pam happened to glance down at the sand. She gasped and the next moment let out a shriek. A big crab was only an inch away from her shoe. Its pincers were open, and as she moved, they caught the edge of it.

"Let go!" Pam cried, waving her foot in the air. She expected that any second he would reach her toes.

Quick as a flash, Rachel grabbed the crab by the back with one hand and snapped the claw with her free fingers until he loosened his hold.

"The horrible creature!" said Pam. "Thanks a million, Rachel."

"I'm glad I could help," the other girl laughed.

Then she said she must go home for lunch. The Hollisters waved good-by and set off for Uncle Russ's house. When they told their mother what Grandma Alden had said, Mrs. Hollister promised to go back with the children as soon as they had finished eating.

Grandma Alden came out to meet them as they walked up the path to her little cottage some time later.

After introductions were made, they all sat down, and Mrs. Hollister opened her purse. She drew out the white box containing the emerald and handed it to Grandma Alden.

"I agree with my children," she said, smiling, "that you should have this."

Grandma Alden took the lid off the box. For a moment she gazed at the lovely green stone. Then she said:

"I have a secret to tell you all. I believe this emerald is part of the pirate treasure which was lost on the *Mystery*."

Everyone stared in amazement.

"Pirate treasure!" the children repeated excitedly.

"Yes," Grandma Alden said, nodding her head emphatically. "Every once in awhile a gem is found on the beach."

"Did you ever see a pirate?" Sue asked, her eyes wide with amazement.

Holly swung her pigtails excitedly as she said, "They're real bad men with swords and they make poor innocent people walk the plank! We know because we had a play in our back yard."

Ricky spoke up quickly. "Yes," he agreed, "and if

the pirates who lost the emerald were as bad as Joey Brill they were terrible mean pirates!"

Grandma Alden looked smilingly from child to child as they poured out their story about the play they had given in Shoreham.

Then their mother said, "Please don't interrupt. Mrs. Alden was about to tell us of the pirate treasure here at Sea Gull Beach."

The children listened excitedly as Grandma Alden related how other valuable gems had been found on the nearby beach.

"Yikes!" exclaimed Ricky, bouncing up and down in his chair. "Then the wrecked ship really must be near here!"

"It does seem like good proof," declared Grandma Alden.

"I have a secret to tell you all."

"There must be other gems where this one was found!" Pete reasoned. "If we look around where this came from, maybe we can find some more."

"Now, that's a bright idea," Grandma Alden nodded approvingly.

"Will you please show us where you got the clay?" Ricky asked impatiently.

"I don't know the exact spot," the elderly woman replied. "I'll have to get in touch with Scowbanger. He brought the clay to me."

Scowbanger! What a strange name! The Hollister children looked at Rachel's grandmother questioningly.

"Grandma Alden," Holly asked, twirling one of her pigtails, "who is Scowbanger?"

CHAPTER 7

Jenny Jump

"WHO is Scowbanger?" Grandma Alden repeated, smiling. "Why he's the best known person in Sea Gull Beach."

"Is that his real name?" Pete asked.

"It's his nickname, which he has had for many years."

The elderly woman explained that the word scowbanger meant a beachcomber. Only this particular scowbanger was a combination beachcomber, fisherman and treasure hunter.

"He's a nice old man," Rachel put in. "And he has a funny beach buggy."

"What's that?" Pam questioned.

Rachel said that Scowbanger's beach buggy was an old car with oversized balloon tires. He drove it up and down the beach, looking for odds and ends washed in by the waves.

"If you haven't been introduced to Scowbanger," Grandma Alden remarked, "you really haven't seen Sea Gull Beach. Rachel, you must take the Hollisters to his shack tomorrow morning."

71

Rachel said she would like to and so arrived directly after breakfast the next day.

"Come on," she said. "We want to catch him before he goes out."

"Wait a second," Ricky begged. "I have to put fresh water in my periwinkle jar."

He ran down to the ocean, scooped up some water into the jar and hurried back to place it in a shady spot on the front porch. Then all the children, including Sue, set off with Rachel.

They walked along the beach awhile, then Rachel led them between two huge dunes and started climbing one from the rear. Reaching the top, she pointed ahead.

"There's Scowbanger's shack over there."

The cabin stood by itself with a fine view of the beach. The children quickened their pace and soon reached the homemade shack. It was a patchwork of driftwood, with two windows, a door, and a crooked little stovepipe chimney sticking out of the roof.

Rachel knocked on the door, calling out, "Scowbanger, are you there?"

"Sure am," a deep voice boomed out.

The door opened and a tall, weatherbeaten man stood before them. He wore white sailor pants and a blue shirt open at the neck. On his head sat a navy and white captain's cap with a tiny gold anchor on the front of it.

Scowbanger's thin, tanned face was covered with

"Well, well, you brought me some new friends."

a fuzzy gray beard and his eyes twinkled as he looked at the callers.

"Well, well, Rachel," he said, "I see you brought me some new friends."

He picked up Sue and set her on his shoulder. "Yo ho ho and a band of pirates! I'll bet these are the Happy Hollisters."

Sue's eyes grew wide as saucers. "How do you know, Mr. Scowbanger?"

"Good news travels fast," he replied. "And I get all the news."

Sue squirmed to get down and said she would like to see Scowbanger's house. He set her on the ground, and they all stepped inside.

What a strange place it was! Odd shaped pieces of driftwood lay everywhere. Beautifully colored sea

73

shells were fastened on the walls. Hanging from the ceiling was a faded white fish net with little starfish dangling on strings from it.

Pete spied a compass on top of a low table in one corner. It looked just like the one that old Mr. Sparr had lent the children for their pirate play in Shoreham. Pete told Scowbanger the story of the lost compass.

"Would you sell me this one," he asked, "so I can give it to Mr. Sparr?"

"That I'll do, me hearty," the man replied. "And I'll make it a bargain, too. I'm due to find another compass soon."

Scowbanger mentioned the price, and Pete took several coins from his pocket. When the boy found he didn't have quite enough, he whispered to Pam, who gave him a couple more. The boy handed the money to Scowbanger and took the compass.

"I'll take this to Mr. Sparr as soon as I get home," Pete declared.

When Ricky was sure he had seen everything in the beachcomber's shack, he asked eagerly, "Will you show us your beach buggy, Scowbanger?"

"And why not?" the man replied. "It's down at the foot of the dune."

They followed him outside, and down the far side of the dune. When they reached the bottom, there stood the funniest jalopy they had ever seen. It was an old type automobile whose fenders and roof had been removed, and it had enormous balloon tires.

"Oh boy! This is keen!" Ricky shouted.

"I call her Jenny Jump," Scowbanger said, patting the side of the beach buggy. "That's because she can leap over sandy gullies like a frog."

The Hollisters laughed as they walked around Jenny Jump.

"May we see it jump?" Holly asked.

"That you can do," came the reply. Scowbanger turned to Pete. "How about you taking Jenny Jump for a spin?"

"Golly, that'd be super!" the boy exclaimed. "You mean I can run it?"

"Easiest thing in the world. Just push or pull, dependin' on which way you want to go."

The jalopy's owner explained that he couldn't be

"Here I go!"

bothered with fancy gear shifts so he had fixed this one to suit himself.

"Push that handle to the front and away you'll go," he instructed Pete. "Then when you want to stop, just say 'Whoa, Jenny!' and pull her back like you'd rein in a horse."

Scowbanger started the motor, which coughed and sputtered noisily, making the whole car tremble.

"Don't worry," he said. "Jenny Jump is only shaking from old age."

Pete hopped into the driver's seat and waved his sisters and brother to step aside.

"Here I go!" he chuckled.

Jenny Jump bucked a couple of times, then chugged off down the sand, gaining speed as she went. The ride was bumpy but Pete thought this was fun. And Jenny did seem to jump the holes in the sand like a frog!

When Pete had gone about a quarter of a mile, he turned the car in a big circle and headed back toward the others. As he drew near the spot, Pete reached down for the shift. Saying softly, "Whoa, Jenny!" he tried to pull the lever back. But it would not budge!

Quickly Pete steered the beach buggy to the right to avoid hitting the group.

"Wow! What'll I do?" Pete thought frantically.

He went up the beach in the other direction, then turned again. As he shot past Scowbanger, the old man cried, "Stop! The others want a ride!"

"I can't!" Pete shouted back.

He decided to turn again. But he cut too sharply. The left front wheel of the car hit a hole in the sand. Jenny Jump lurched violently. Pete knew it was going to overturn and flung himself from the driver's seat just in time! The old jalopy flip flopped and landed upside down with the wheels still spinning madly. Scowbanger rushed up and stopped the motor.

After jumping from the speeding buggy, Pete had rolled over and over on the beach, but now scrambled to his feet.

"Did I ruin your beach buggy?" he asked fearfully.

"No. No. Now don't you worry," Scowbanger said. "I guess Jenny Jump doesn't take to new riders."

As the old man stroked his stubbly beard, Pete told him about the tight shift.

Scowbanger smiled. "Yeah, Jenny does freeze up once in a while," he explained. "Well, children, we'll have to set her on her feet again. Grab one side here. One, two, three—heave ho!"

As the jalopy bounced back on its wheels, the beachcomber said, "You've had your exercise for the day, Jenny," and added, "What say we sit down and have a chat, boys and girls?"

"Will you tell us about pirates and the treasures you've found?" Ricky asked, as they seated themselves.

Scowbanger tilted his captain's hat back on his head and looked intently into the faces of the children.

77

They searched all through the sand.

"Now I'm glad you want to hear that," he chuckled. "Once upon a time, there were plenty of pirates in this area, and I'll bet you they left a great deal of treasure, too."

"Have you found any of it?" Holly questioned eagerly.

"I reckon I have. I've collected everything from jewelry to old coins," Scowbanger replied. "The pirates prob'ly dropped 'em."

The treasure hunter winked one eye and continued, "But there're two ways to find treasures. The right way and the wrong way. I'm against diving down under the water to hunt for old wrecks. Let the sea give up her treasures when she will!"

The Hollisters were somewhat mystified by this and asked Scowbanger what he meant.

"Well, I let the sea work for me," he went on. "When she's ready to give up her treasures, she'll do it, but not a second before."

Sue looked up at Scowbanger and asked, "Did the sea give up our green lighthouse stone?"

When the old man asked what she meant, Pete told the story of the emerald they had returned to Grandma Alden, and that she had said it was in the clay Scowbanger had brought her.

"Hm," the beachcomber said. "That's a right good find."

Pete asked Scowbanger if he would take them to the spot where he had found the clay.

"That I'll do," the old man replied, rising and stretching his long legs. "Come, follow me."

He led them down the beach to another dune where a big hole had been scooped out of its sandy side.

"Here's the place that good clay came from," he said. "Too bad there's none of it left. You children might look around and see if you can find any more emeralds."

"Oh let's!" Holly cried eagerly.

Digging with little sticks, they searched through the sand and pebbles. Finally Holly shouted:

"Look at this!"

When her brothers and sisters and Rachel rushed up to her, they found that she was holding what looked like the lid of a brass box. On it was a design of flowered figures.

Pete raced after the man.

"It's beautiful!" Pam cried. "Maybe it's part of a jewel box!"

"Do you suppose the rest of it's hidden around here?" Ricky asked excitedly. "And emeralds are in it?"

As he said this, a sound above them distracted Pam's attention. She glanced upward. At the top of the dune she saw a head duck quickly out of sight.

"Somebody's watching us!" she told the others.

Scowbanger's eyes snapped. "I'll bet it's one of those treasure hunters. They've been following me around for days. But I won't tell 'em a thing!"

"Let's chase that spy!" Pete said determinedly.

He climbed the dune quickly, with the others following. Pete was just in time to see a man disappear into a pine thicket. He raced after him. But in a little while the fellow was out of sight, and Pete gave up.

As he turned back, Ricky and Scowbanger met him.

"He got away," Pete reported.

They walked back to the clay pit, picking up various members of their party on the way. Rachel had lost her sandal and was hunting for it in the shifting sand. Pam had stayed behind with Sue who could not keep up with the others.

As they all began to discuss who the eavesdropper might have been and whether he would dig for the jewel box, Pam suddenly looked around, her eyes taking on a frightened look.

"Where's Holly?" she cried.

No one knew. Pete climbed the dune and gazed in all directions. He called down that he could not see their sister.

"Oh, dear!" Sue wailed. "Holly's lost!"

CHAPTER 8

A Nest Robber

AT ONCE a search started for the missing Holly. The girls ran along the beach near the water. None of them dared say out loud the dreadful thought that had come to them: Holly might have been caught by a wave and swept into the water.

Scowbanger and the boys hurried to the top of the dune because the old man was sure he had seen Holly up there. She was nowhere in sight and did not answer their shouts.

"What'll we do?" Ricky asked, struggling to keep back the tears. He was very close to Holly and if anything had happened to her—

"Maybe she went home," Scowbanger suggested, seeing the worried looks of both boys.

But Holly had not gone home. At this moment she was lost and trapped deep in the pine woods back of the dune.

After she had seen Pete give up the chase, Holly had spied an extra large pine cone and decided to look for more.

"They'll be nice to hang on our Christmas tree next winter," she told herself.

Walking along slowly, hunting for perfect cones, the girl smiled suddenly. The trees reminded her of little gnarled gnomes which she had read about in fairy tales. Their trunks and branches were twisted, she supposed, from the high winds and severe storms.

As she went deeper into the woods, Holly was delighted with the lovely scent and the thick carpet of pine needles. How wonderful it was to walk on them!

She kept pulling cones from the trees and picking them up from the ground. Soon both her hands were so full, she had a hard time holding all the cones.

"If I only had a bag to put these in," she thought.

Suddenly she saw a withered vine trailing along the ground. This gave her an idea. Stripping the vine of its brown leaves, Holly tied one cone after another to it. Soon she had a whole string of them.

"I guess I have plenty," she decided, and turned around to retrace her steps to the beach.

Holly thought it would be no trouble at all to find her way back, since she could hear the faint murmur of the ocean in the distance. But after a while she stopped. Now the sound seemed to come from all directions at once. Which way was the ocean?

Holly walked first in one direction, then another. But she did not come to the edge of the woods.

"I know," Holly told herself. "The sun will show me which way to go."

When she looked up, though, the sun was directly overhead, and gave her no help in finding the right direction.

Which way WAS the ocean?

Holly was determined to remain calm, but could not keep from worrying a little. She began to walk faster through the pine woods, dragging the cones behind her. Suddenly she stubbed her toe.

"Ouch!" she cried and looked down.

Her foot was stuck beneath a twisted root, which had been hidden by the soft pine needles. Holly tried to free herself, but the more she pulled and tugged, the tighter her foot became wedged in the odd root formation.

"I'm trapped!" she thought excitedly. "How— how will I ever get out of here?"

Now Holly was frightened. She dropped her string of pine cones and cupped her hands to her mouth.

"Pete! Pam! Scowbanger!" she shouted.

When no reply came, she waited a few seconds and then cried out again.

"Oh, if they could only hear me!" she wailed when still there was no answer.

A tear ran down Holly's nose and her chin began to quiver. She tugged again to get her foot out, but it hurt her dreadfully to pull it! She *must* get help.

"Pete! Pam!" she called out with all her might.

Was that only a faint echo she heard? Or was it somebody answering her call?

Holly shouted again. It hadn't been an echo! Somebody was calling her name. Pam's voice!

In a few moments Pete, Pam and Ricky burst into sight. Holly was so relieved to see them she started laughing and crying at the same time.

"Oh, Holly, what happened to you?"

"Oh, Holly, what happened to you?" Pam exclaimed, running up to her.

Her sister showed how her foot had become caught in the scraggly roots. Pete unfastened her sandal, then gently eased Holly's foot out as Ricky pulled the roots apart. Then the sandal was put back on.

"We—we thought maybe you'd drowned!" Pam said a bit hysterically.

"I'm terribly sorry I worried you all," Holly apologized, picking up the pine cones and hurrying after the others to the beach.

How relieved Sue, Rachel and Scowbanger were to see Holly!

"Must be mighty hard keeping track of a big family like yours," the beachcomber grinned.

Pam thought the children should return home, and Scowbanger said that he would walk along with them part of the way. Presently they came to a place where the shore line curved. As they rounded a little point, the group saw a boy halfway up a dune. He was bending over something set into the sand among a clump of bayberry bushes.

"Hey there!" Scowbanger called. "What are you doing?"

When the boy looked around, Rachel exclaimed, "That's Homer Ruffly!"

"The scamp!" Scowbanger cried angrily. "He's stealing eggs from a tern's nest!"

When Homer heard the beachcomber's remark, he

86

Homer scooped the eggs into his cap.

scooped out several of the bird's eggs into his cap and
started up at a quick pace over the dunes.

"Come back here!" Scowbanger demanded in a
stern voice. "It's against the law to steal terns' eggs."

But Homer paid no attention. He broke into a fast
run and scooted out of sight before anybody had a
chance to chase him.

"What a bothersome rascal he is," Scowbanger
muttered. "Takes after his father, all right. Mr. Ruffly's bragging that he'll find the pirate treasure."

Soon they reached Uncle Russ's house, so Pam invited Scowbanger to come in. When she introduced
him, Uncle Russ said:

"Scowbanger and I are old acquaintances. By the
way," he asked the beachcomber, "do you still have
that old diving outfit?"

Scowbanger had raked in a diving suit from the waves years before and never found the owner. The suit was still in good condition.

"Would you do me a big favor—put on the suit and go down off our dock?" Uncle Russ asked him. "I'd like to make some sketches for my comic strip."

Scowbanger laughed and said he guessed he'd be funny all right. He would do it.

"When do you want me?" the beachcomber asked.

"Could you be here at three this afternoon?"

"That I can," he replied and departed for his shack.

At three o'clock sharp, Scowbanger drove up in Jenny Jump. He stopped the beach buggy alongside the lone pier where Uncle Russ had asked him to come. The beachcomber carried the diving suit out to where the Hollisters were standing at the end.

"All set?" the cartoonist asked him.

"I am," the old man replied.

As he tried to wriggle into the diving suit, Pete sprang forward to help him. Before Scowbanger put on the helmet, he pointed to the hose and the machine at the end of it.

"Somebody will have to keep track of this air pump," he said. "Be very careful that I get enough air while I'm walking on the bottom of the ocean."

"Don't worry," Uncle Russ assured him. "You just show us how to operate the pump."

After hearing the instructions, Mr. Hollister felt certain he could manipulate it.

Scowbanger climbed down slowly.

"I'd better take my position in the boat," Uncle Russ said. "Come on, Pete."

The cartoonist had rented a glass bottom rowboat which was tied to a post under the pier.

Pete was to keep it steady with the oars while his uncle sketched. The two climbed down a ladder and sat down in the boat.

"All ready!" Uncle Russ called.

Scowbanger now clamped on a funny round helmet. Then, waving to his audience, he climbed slowly down the ladder.

He kept watching Uncle Russ for instructions. The artist was working fast. Every once in a while he would hold up his hand for the diver to pause or to hold out an arm or a leg.

Scowbanger caught on quickly to the idea of making the pictures funny. He bent over for a couple of minutes, then he stood with just one hand and one foot on the ladder, pretending to be falling.

"This is like a circus," Ricky cried gleefully.

Finally Scowbanger reached the water. Everyone watched, fascinated, as first his feet disappeared, then his legs. Soon only the big round helmet could be seen. The next second Scowbanger was out of sight.

"Oh, is he all right?" Sue asked, clutching her mother's hand.

"Yes, dear," Mrs. Hollister replied, and looked down to where air bubbles from the diving suit's exhaust were appearing on the surface of the water.

Uncle Russ was sketching furiously. He seemed to be able to look through the floor of the glass-bottomed boat and draw on the pad before him all at the same time!

Suddenly the artist began to chuckle. "Scowbanger just hugged a big fish and it slapped him on the helmet with its tail!" he called up.

The Hollisters laughed. But suddenly they stopped as they heard running footsteps. Homer Ruffly was coming along the dock toward them.

"Hey, is your diver looking for the pirate treasure?" he asked.

"No, he's not," Ricky replied.

"Then what is he looking for?" Homer wanted to know.

Ricky explained that his Uncle Russ was only making sketches of the diver. Homer seemed satisfied, at least for a few seconds. Then he walked over to the air pump.

"Say, this isn't the way you work a pump," he said, touching the apparatus. "My father showed me how."

Mr. Hollister called a warning to the boy to take his hands off, but it was too late. Homer had turned a valve on the pump. A second later there was a violent tug on the line extending down to Scowbanger.

"Something's gone wrong!" Ricky cried.

CHAPTER 9

Walking Under Water

"QUICK! Haul him up!" Uncle Russ shouted, as Scowbanger continued to jerk on the line.

The two Hollister girls, with their father and Ricky, hauled the diver to the surface and pulled him to the dock. Pam quickly unscrewed the helmet and her father lifted it off Scowbanger's head. The poor old man was only half conscious.

"See what you did!" Holly scolded Homer, who was too frightened to say a word.

"You naughty boy! You nearly drowned him," Sue added, shaking a chubby finger.

While Mr. Hollister held Scowbanger upright, the others removed his diving suit. Then they laid him on the dock. Mr. Hollister massaged his wrists, and Mrs. Hollister bathed his head with cool water. Presently Scowbanger said he felt like himself once more.

"Somebody shut off my air," he said, looking around accusingly. Seeing Homer, he cried, "I'll bet you did!"

Homer said that he had not meant to hurt Scowbanger.

"All right, boy," Scowbanger said, "just so long

as you didn't do it intentionally. But hereafter keep your hands off other people's property!"

He turned to Uncle Russ. "Did you make enough sketches?"

"I'd like to do a few more," the cartoonist replied, "but you mustn't go down again."

Pete, who was on the dock now, said, "How about letting me go down this time?"

"A boy has never used this outfit," Scowbanger replied. "But if your father's willing, it's fine with me."

Mr. Hollister exchanged a few words with his wife, then said if Scowbanger would supervise the operation, Pete might go down in the diving suit.

"Yikes!" Ricky cried. "I wish I was you!"

Mr. Hollister lifted the helmet off.

Pete was ready in a few minutes, but he had trouble lifting his weighted feet as he moved to the ladder. Scowbanger started the air pump, and the boy gradually descended into the water, as his brother and sisters looked on enviously.

When Pete touched bottom, he began to walk forward. He was surprised how much easier it was than on land.

"I wish I could find a pirate ship or a treasure," he thought.

But at first he saw nothing except the fish that swam around him. Then among some plants growing in the sand, he spied an old boot. He picked it up, wondering if Uncle Russ would think this a funny picture to sketch.

At this moment there was a tug on his line, which was a signal for the boy to start upward. He walked back to the steps and climbed to the dock. When the watchers saw the boot, they laughed.

"But maybe there's a treasure in it," Ricky said hopefully.

"Oh yeah?" Homer sneered.

Nevertheless he thrust his hand deep into the toe of the boot. Then a funny look came over his face and he yelled:

"Ow! Something stung me!" He jerked out his hand, which had a red welt on it.

Ricky picked up the fallen boot, held it upside down and shook it. Out fell a baby jellyfish.

"Some treasure!" the boy said in disgust.

94

"Some treasure!" Ricky said in disgust.

Meanwhile the diving suit was taken off Pete, but before he had a chance to tell of his adventure, Homer whined:

"Somebody do something for me. My hand hurts."

"Come back to the house with me," Mrs. Hollister said, "and I'll put some lotion on it."

As she and Homer walked off the dock, the others helped Scowbanger put the diving suit in his jalopy. Uncle Russ thanked him, and the old man drove off.

When Pete walked home, he noticed that the wind was rising.

"Good kite weather," he thought.

That evening he worked with the supplies he had brought from The Trading Post and by bedtime had put together a large, good-looking kite.

"By morning the glue'll be dry, and I can fly it," he told himself.

Pete was awake early, put on his bathing trunks and a sweater and went to the kitchen. After eating some fruit, cereal and milk, the boy wrote a short note, saying where he would be. Leaving it on the table, Pete picked up his kite and ran outside.

The kite looked even better in the daylight, and he was eager to see how it would fly. Reaching the beach, he saw three other boys about his age already flying kites.

"I suppose they're practicing for the contest," Pete said, walking up to them.

The boys looked up and smiled. They resembled one another so much with their turned-up noses and black curly hair, Pete was sure they were brothers.

"Hello, I'm Pete Hollister from Shoreham."

"Hi! I'm Tom Fraser," the tallest boy replied. "These are my brothers Tim and Terry." He grinned. "People call us the Fraser steps. We're twelve, eleven and ten years old. We live at Sea Gull Beach all the year around."

"When did you come?" Terry asked Pete.

"We just arrived. My Uncle Russ Hollister has a house here. Maybe you've heard of him. He's a cartoonist."

"Oh, is he your uncle?" Tim said. "His comic about Airman Alphonse is the funniest thing I ever read. Maybe we can meet him."

"Sure thing," Pete smiled. "Come up to the house

any time." He pointed out the one which Uncle Russ had rented. Then eying the Fraser boys' kites, he went on, "They're swell. Did you make them?"

"Yes," Tom answered. "We're entering them in the contest. It's on the seventeenth. Have you heard about it?"

Pete said he had and wanted to go in it.

"The prizes are nifty," Terry told him. "We hope to win one this year. Last summer not a single local boy got one."

"And were our faces red!" Tom laughed. "The fellows in our school are determined not to let the visitors take all the prizes."

"Well, good luck," said Pete. "But leave one prize for me, will you?" Then he added, "Say, if you fel-

"We hope to win a prize this year."

lows have lived here all your lives, you must know
something about the pirate ship, the Mystery."

The brothers laughed, and Tom said, "Oh, that's
an old story around here. People have been looking
for it for years. Every summer a new outfit comes with
a diver."

"But no one's found out a thing," Terry spoke
up.

"You mean they haven't even turned up a clue?"
Pete asked.

"Nothing that you could say was part of the Mystery. Of course, people are always finding souvenirs
buried on the beach, but they probably didn't come
from the pirate ship."

Pete thought this over a few moments as he got his
kite ready to fly. But he decided not to be disheartened
by the Frasers' talk. Somebody at some time had to
find the Mystery. It could just as well be the Hollisters
as anyone else!

"I'd better get started flying my kite to see how it
works—if I hope to win a prize," he laughed.

The talk turned again to the contest. Tom said that
children came from miles around to take part in the
annual event. Sea Gull Beach was crowded with
people on that day.

The four boys walked to the top of the dune where
the wind was exceptionally strong. Soon it was rus-
tling the kite paper, as they let out the strings, foot by
foot. For the first time, Pete noticed that Tom's had
a clown painted on his. Tim's was shaped like a pig,

98

The kites soared high over the dunes.

and Terry's resembled an airplane. When he asked them why, Tom said they figured there might be more of a chance to win a prize with an unusual type.

"This is neat fun!" Pete said as the kites sailed into the air.

"Wait till you see a hundred of 'em flying all at the same time!" Tim told him.

"I can hardly wait for the seventeenth," Pete remarked, letting out his string very fast.

All four of the kites now looked like birds, soaring high in the sky over the dunes. Then suddenly Tom's began to dip, first in one direction and then the other.

"I think one of the sticks is broken," he observed. "I'd better reel her in before she crashes."

He wound up the string as fast as he could, and,

in a few moments, the kite gently touched the ground, not far from where he was standing.

"It's a broken stick, all right," Pete said, running over to examine it. "I'll help you fix it, Tom."

He glanced about for a place to tie his own kite string. Seeing a stout bush, he went over and tied the string tightly. Then he ran back to where Tom was sitting in the tall dune grass.

"Let's splice this broken stick together," Pete suggested.

"Okay. Thanks."

While Tom held the broken ends of the stick firmly together, Pete tied a string around and around them. Just as he finished the job, Tom glanced up and said:

"Here comes that Ruffly kid again. I wish he wouldn't bother us."

"So do I," Pete agreed.

But Homer walked up to them, looking very important. "What are you doing?" he asked.

"Repairing my kite stick," Tom replied without looking up.

"Why don't you make 'em so they can't break?"

Pete noticed the color rush up into his friend's cheeks, but Tom held his temper and did not reply.

When Homer realized he could not ruffle Tom, he turned to Pete. "I suppose you think you've got the best kite at Sea Gull Beach," he said.

"We'll see when the contest is held," Pete replied as he finished mending the split stick.

"Hey, where's your kite?" Homer asked suddenly, looking around the dune.

Before Pete could reply, Homer glanced into the sky. He spied Pete's kite.

"Not bad," he said softly.

When Homer saw the kite string tied to the bush, he ran over to it.

"Hey, let that alone!" Pete shouted.

But Homer already had untied the string and was holding it in his hand.

"Hang on to that tight," Pete warned, running over to the boy.

But just then a strong gust made an extra hard tug on the string. It slipped from Homer's hands!

"Grab it!" Pete yelled, as the ball of string bounced and tumbled along the ground.

He ran after the string, too. But every time they tried to grasp it, the string yanked out of their reach. In a moment, the kite headed out toward the ocean.

"I'll never get it now!" Pete thought woefully.

CHAPTER 10

A Ruined Castle

HOMER gave up and stopped running after the kite. But Pete continued to chase the fast-moving string across the dunes, then down on the beach.

"Crickets," thought Pete as he raced along. "If only the wind would stop blowing!"

Its course had changed, fortunately, and now the kite was being carried along above the sand instead of over the water. Pete hoped to catch the kite before the wind might change again and carry it out to sea.

Hearing a chug chug, Pete turned and saw Scowbanger driving toward him in his beach buggy. When the old man saw what was happening, he speeded up, and soon was alongside the racing boy.

"Hop in!" he shouted, slowing down a little. "Maybe we can catch that string."

Pete jumped in and off they went after the leaping, bounding ball of string. Pete leaned far out and finally managed to touch it but could not grasp the string.

Scowbanger tried to run over it and anchor the now tiny ball but he missed. He stopped and Pete leaped out. As he made a final grab, the mischievous wind blew it away. In a second, kite and string were over the water.

The boy waded in but the chase was hopeless. The string was whisked far out into deep water. In a few moments the string was soaking wet and the kite settled down onto the sea. Soon it disappeared under the waves.

"Too bad, Pete," Scowbanger said. "We nearly had it."

By this time the Fraser boys had reeled in their kites and come up. They too said they were sorry, but that Homer had gone off without a word. Then Terry added:

"Maybe it's just as well you lost the kite, Pete. We didn't want to tell you before, but you don't stand much chance in the contest if your kite isn't sort of unusual."

"You mean like yours?" Pete asked.

"That's right. Think up something original."

"Say, fellows," said Scowbanger suddenly, "do you want to go on a beachcombin' expedition with me?"

"Sure. Thanks," they all answered.

"Then come on," he said. "I'll introduce you to a place that never fails me."

The four boys climbed aboard, and the beach buggy started off.

"Where are we going?" Pete asked.

"First I'm going to show you where pirates sometimes landed."

The beachcomber drove along the shore, dodging

pieces of driftwood and bouncing over little gullies in the sand. Presently they came to a place where the beach was very narrow. The shore line curved inland a short distance, and the boys were surprised to see a perfect little harbor.

"The marsh land behind this spot keeps the summer visitors out," Scowbanger said with a wink. "But the pirates didn't mind. They brought their boats in here and dropped anchor."

As they drove slowly along, all of them kept their eyes open for articles of value the waves might have brought in.

"There's a crate of oranges!" Tim cried. "I'll get it for you, Scowbanger."

Just as he was stowing it aboard, Pete spotted a box wedged between two small rocks. Excitedly he dashed

The beach buggy started off.

over and opened it. Had some pirate—? Then he boy laughed. The box contained a sodden shoe cleaning kit.

All this time Scowbanger had been poking in the sand and come up with a strange assortment: three beautiful shells, a turtle with a date on its back and a queer shaped bottle.

"There's a note in the bottle!" Tom cried.

Scowbanger dug the cork out with a penknife and opened the note. It read:

"*Bet you got all excited when you saw this, Scowbanger. I did it for a joke. H.*"

"Homer!" the old man cried. "I'll thrash that kid when I get hold of him!"

They climbed into the beach buggy again. On the way to the next stop, Scowbanger told them the story of two pirate ships which were found in the cove a long time ago. No one was on them.

"The ships stayed here for several years, I understand," Scowbanger went on, "until the finders sailed away in them."

"Who were they?" Terry asked.

"Four boys like yourselves," the beachcomber replied. "When they grew up, they became merchant seamen and sailed the pirate vessels all over the world."

"I'd like to do that," Tom said.

"Me too," the others added.

"You know," said Scowbanger as he drove along the water front, "there were once Indians here too.

"Hey, look at this!" he shouted.

Sometimes I find souvenirs where the village was. Want to see it?"

"You bet," Pete answered for all the boys.

The old man turned inland and climbed a shallow dune. Soon they came to a high level spot near a small stand of dwarf pine trees. Scowbanger stopped and turned off the motor.

"Here we are, boys. Do you want to get out? Maybe you can find some arrowheads."

The four stepped to the ground. Pete picked up a stick and began to probe into the fine soil. In a moment, he dug up a small flat rock. He was about to toss it aside when some carving on it caught his eye.

"Hey, look at this!" he shouted.

On one side was a crude carving of a deer, and on the other, the outline of a soaring sea gull.

106

Scowbanger was excited. "This is a fine piece! It's Indian art work!"

"Then I shouldn't keep it," Pete said. "It ought to be in a museum."

"That's right," Scowbanger said. "There's one in town."

Terry offered to take it there, as he lived nearby and Pete handed it to him.

As they walked toward the jalopy, Pete said, "Fellows, the carved sea gull gives me an idea. I think I'll make a kite to look like it."

"That would be different, all right," Tom agreed. "I don't remember anyone flying a kite like that."

When Pete reached home, his family looked relieved.

"From your note," his mother said, "I thought you'd be right back."

But after she and the others heard his adventures, they forgot about being worried.

"We couldn't go look at the pirate ship hunters till you came," Ricky pouted. "Come on!"

He was out the door in a flash and the others followed. Uncle Russ led them along the beach until they came to the mouth of a river. A short distance inside it a barge was moored, and there was considerable activity on it.

"Oh, I see a diver," Pam called out. "He's just starting down."

"The old timers around here don't think Mr. Ruffly's going to find the sunken ship, the *Mystery*, at this spot," Uncle Russ said.

"You mean we might find it somewhere else?" Ricky asked excitedly.

"You might," his uncle grinned. "I wish I had some clues for you, but I guess you'll just have to hunt for them yourself."

"Better wait until after lunch," his mother teased.

They watched the work on the barge a little while, then returned home. The children spent the afternoon on the beach swimming, digging and trying to figure out how to pick up a clue to the wrecked pirate ship.

One by one they went back to the house until only Mrs. Hollister, Holly and Sue were left. The two little girls begged to stay a little longer, saying they would only play on the sand. As it was low tide, their mother consented, saying she would run up to the house to start supper and come back for them in a little while. She spoke to the lifeguard who promised to keep an eye on them.

After Mrs. Hollister had gone, Sue and Holly walked down to the shore where a little neck of land jutted out into the water.

"Let's go out there and make a fairy castle," Holly suggested to her sister.

"That'll be fun," Sue replied. "A castle right out in the middle of the ocean."

Both girls ran back to get their pails and shovels, then went to the end of the little peninsula.

Soon a sand castle began to take shape under their busy hands. Sue picked up a small sea shell and with it pressed steps into the castle from the bottom to the top.

"Now the fairies can get up to the tower without flying," the little girl giggled happily.

When the castle was complete, a small wave rolled along the flat sand and lapped at the steps.

"Let's move back a ways and build another one," Holly suggested.

They made the next one larger with a bigger tower and more windows in it.

"I'm going to dig a secret tunnel under the castle," Sue declared eagerly.

She lay flat and wiggled her hand through the sand

A sand castle began to take shape.

as far as she could reach. Then she skipped to the other side of the castle and started another opening. In a few minutes, her fingers came to the other part of the tunnel.

"I did it!" Sue exclaimed happily.

But as she stood up, another wavelet curled along the sand and filled the tunnel with water.

"If I had a boat it could sail right under the castle," the little girl remarked. "Holly, wouldn't that be a good thing for pirates to do?"

"Yes," said her sister, who had stuffed her red handkerchief into the sand on the top of the tower.

"That looks nice," Sue commented. "We ought to— Look!" she cried suddenly.

A big wave was rolling in. The next instant it soaked the girls and ruined the castle completely.

"Oh dear, see what's happened!" Sue sighed unhappily.

Holly stood up and looked out over the ocean. "I know why it happened. The tide's coming in," she said. "We'd better go home as fast as we can. We don't want to be caught out here."

The girls picked up their pails and started hand in hand along the little strip of sand. But they stopped short as Sue cried out:

"Oh, Holly, look! The ocean—it—it's all around us! What'll we do?"

CHAPTER 11

The Lifeguard's Story

THERE were few bathers on the beach, and the lifeguard was not in sight. In the distance, Holly and Sue could see their mother coming, but now the little strip of sand was almost covered with water.

"We'll have to run through the waves," Holly said.

"No, no! I'm afraid," Sue cried. "Don't leave me."

Holly did not know what to do. She could not leave her little sister alone, but she must think of a way to get back to the beach. An idea suddenly came to Holly.

"I'll pickaback you, Sue," she offered and bent down.

Sue climbed up, then Holly started to walk through the water. But it was much deeper than she had thought. Fearful, she turned back to the higher spot.

Sue was terribly frightened, now. She clung to her sister and began to cry. Just then Holly saw a boat not far away. A girl was rowing it. Holly jumped up and down, waving her hands frantically.

The girl rowed faster. Suddenly Holly exclaimed joyously, "Sue! It's Rachel!"

In a moment she pulled up alongside them. Holly

111

helped Sue into the boat and then jumped in after her.

"Oh, Rachel, you're wonderful!" Holly said.

"I was terribly scared," Sue added.

"It's a lucky thing I decided to row in this direction," Rachel declared as she turned the boat toward the shore.

Holly and Sue were astonished at the way she could keep it from upsetting in the waves. Finally they came to the beach and the three girls hopped out. Then Holly helped Rachel pull the rowboat high up on the sand.

Mrs. Hollister rushed up to them. Holly told the story of their rescue to her mother, who was amazed to learn that the lifeguard was not around. At this moment, he came running back to the beach and explained that a woman bather had been taken ill and he had rushed her to a doctor in his car.

"I'm glad your girls are safe," he said, after hearing the story, and praised Rachel for bringing them in.

He introduced himself as Bill Brown and asked who the Hollisters were and where they were staying. When he heard they were relatives of the cartoonist, he said:

"I enjoy Russ's drawings. Wouldn't miss looking them up in the papers. He's hoping to get some sketches of the old pirate ship the Mystery when Mr. Ruffly hauls her up, I hear."

"Yes," said Holly. "Only we think maybe we'll find it in a different place."

Holly waved her hands frantically.

"Really?" Bill Brown asked, smiling. "Have you some secret information?"

"We found an emerald that might have been part of the pirates' treasure," Holly replied, "and it wasn't near the river."

By this time the other Hollister children had come up and met the lifeguard. Pam asked him if he knew the true story of the *Mystery*.

"There are all sorts of tales about it," Bill Brown said. "The most likely one is this:

"One winter, over a hundred years ago, the pirates were being chased by a government vessel and ran in here to hide. It foundered on a sand bar somewhere on the beach."

"Just like in our pirate play," Pam said excitedly, and told him briefly about it.

Then Bill went on, "Just as the *Mystery* hit the sand bar, a blizzard came up. It lasted two days and wrecked the ship. Only one man escaped alive, but he was found wandering on the beach out of his mind and died shortly afterward. When the weather cleared, the *Mystery* was gone!"

"And nobody knows where?" Pete asked.

"No. Some folks around here even say she was a ghost ship and never did exist," Bill Brown answered. "My own idea is that part of it washed out to sea, and the rest is buried under the sand here. Well, if you children find it, I hope you'll locate the treasure!"

The lifeguard said good-by and walked off down the beach. Rachel also left, but promised to be over early in the morning to go treasure hunting with her new friends.

When the Hollisters reached the house, Ricky, who was in the lead, suddenly gave a whoop.

"Who took my jar of periwinkles?" he demanded.

Everyone stared. There was no doubt about it. The jar was gone from the spot where it had stood in a corner of the porch.

"I didn't touch it," said Pete.

"Nor I," Pam added.

When the others also said they had not touched the jar, Ricky asked his father and Uncle Russ. Neither of them had moved the periwinkles.

"Then somebody stole my periwinkles!" Ricky declared.

Uncle Russ felt sorry for him and asked if he and

114

Pete would like to go aquaplaning the next morning.

"I have a friend who owns a small motorboat, and he often takes people out on the river or the ocean," he said.

"It sounds keen," Pete grinned. "I've never stood on an aquaplane and been pulled along the water."

His uncle made a date to meet Mr. Trask at eleven o'clock. When they reached the pier, the jolly skipper was all ready for them. Uncle Russ showed his nephews how to slip their feet into the loops on the beginners' planes and how to hold the ropes.

"Ricky, do you want to try it first?" Mr. Trask asked.

"Oh, yes," the boy said eagerly.

Suddenly Ricky lost his balance.

The boat started off with Ricky holding on tight as the plane skimmed along the water. Then suddenly Ricky lost his balance. Off he went. Mr. Trask picked him up, and they came back to the dock.

Pete was next. Since he was used to skiing, the boy was able to stay on the aquaplane for a long ride. Finally Mr. Trask signaled that he was going to turn around.

Poor Pete was not ready for this. Suddenly his left foot came out of the strap. He lost his balance and went over.

To the boy's dismay his right foot did not pull out of the strap. He hit the water with a smack and was dragged through it at a fast clip!

Mr. Trask looked back and was horrified to see what had happened. He did not dare stop for fear Pete would hit the boat and be injured. And if he cut the speed too slowly, the boy might drown.

Fate stepped in. Pete's foot suddenly came out of the strap. He was free!

It seemed to Pete as if he could not breathe. But he managed to turn on his back and stay afloat until Mr. Trask swerved his boat around and steered alongside the boy. He reached down and hoisted him aboard.

"That was a close one," Mr. Trask declared. "Are you all right?"

"Oh, sure," Pete answered, but he was very quiet during the ride to the dock.

Uncle Russ and Ricky were mighty glad to see him

116

and glad to learn he had not been injured or swallowed a lot of briny water.

"We'd better go home," Uncle Russ said, "so you can rest, Pete."

When they reached the house, the brothers learned that Pam and Rachel had gone off to hunt again for a clue to the Mystery. Right now the two girls were inspecting a sand dune which Rachel had never noticed. One section of it was yellowish in color.

"I think this is ocher-colored clay, and it makes pretty pottery," Rachel said. "I'm sure my grandmother would love to have some."

"Then let's get it now," Pam suggested. "There's an old paper bag over by those bushes."

As she went for it, Rachel said, "The cleanest clay's up top. Let's get that."

The dune was very steep at this point, so the girls had to climb up slowly. They finally made it and started to scoop up the pretty sand.

"I wonder why nobody ever found this clay before," Pam said, putting some of it into the bag.

"Probably because the wind just uncovered it," Rachel answered. "Wind does funny things to sand. Sometimes it blows so hard one dune will get much higher in a little while and another one get lower."

"Then there's no telling what might have happened to the Mystery," Pam reflected. "It could have been completely covered in a short time."

"That's right," Rachel agreed. "And a big storm with a lot of wind might uncover it, too."

She began to roll very fast.

"Wouldn't that be wonder—?"

Pam never finished the sentence for at that moment she stepped back too far at the edge of the dune and lost her balance.

She gave a little scream as she began to roll very fast down the side.

"Oh!" she cried.

Pam reached out her hands to clutch at whatever she could find to break her fall. But tufts of grass merely pulled out. She tumbled over and over, skinning her knees and scraping her arms.

"I—I mustn't hit my head on a stone!" Pam told herself, knowing there were some rocks at this point on the beach.

All at once her fingers touched a piece of wood

118

which stuck up a few inches in the slope of the dune. She grabbed for it. The stick stopped her for a moment, then it pulled out and she tumbled farther down. Reaching the bottom of the dune, still holding on to the strange stick, Pam gazed at it in amazement.

"Rachel!" she cried out. "This is part of an old oar. And it has letters on it—MYS. Do you suppose it could be from the pirate ship *Mystery*?"

CHAPTER 12

A Tussle on the Sand

RACHEL slid down the side of the sand dune to where Pam was holding the piece of oar with the letters MYS.

"It's a wonderful clue!" she cried excitedly. "Maybe the old pirate ship is buried right here!"

"Let's get everybody and start digging!" Pam said, jumping up.

But before they had a chance to set off, a voice cried for them to stop and Homer Ruffly dashed up to them from the rear.

"I heard what you said!" he cried out. "You can't take that oar!"

"And why not?" Pam asked. "I found it."

"You can't have it, because—because," Homer faltered, "because I put it there."

"I don't believe you," Rachel said angrily. "Why don't you stay where your father's looking for the treasure?"

"I can do what I like!" Homer flared. "And listen, my father has a right to dig any place he wants to. And that's more than you or the Hollisters or anybody else has."

"What do you mean?" Pam demanded.

"The mayor of Sea Gull Beach gave my father permission," Homer replied. "But what would this summer resort look like if everybody who came here dug the place up?"

Homer puffed out his chest importantly as he gave his little speech which the girls knew he had heard some grownup say. Nevertheless, there might be something to it. Maybe the Hollisters shouldn't hunt for the Mystery without permission from the mayor.

"I'll ask Uncle Russ," Pam thought.

During the past few moments, she had not been holding very tightly to the old oar. Homer noticed this and quick as a wink he grabbed it and began to run.

"You can't have that!" Pam yelled.

Both girls set out in pursuit. All three children were fleet-footed. But Homer, who wore sneakers, had the advantage. The soles of Pam's and Rachel's sandals were smooth and slipped in the sand. Homer got way ahead.

Halfway to the river, Pam saw Pete and Ricky coming up the beach. As loudly as she could, the girl cried out:

"Pete! Ricky! Stop Homer!"

Though her voice did not carry to her brothers, they sensed that something was wrong. The girls seemed to be chasing Homer who was carrying a stick of some sort in his hand.

As a matter of fact, the boys were looking for

Homer themselves. Ricky had a little score to settle with him! The two boys ran up to Homer and caught hold of him.

"Let me go!" he shouted. "I—I have to take this to my father right away."

"Hold him!" Pam cried.

In a few seconds she and Rachel caught up to the others. Ricky was just saying:

"Homer, you're a mean boy. You're cruel, too. You took my jar of periwinkles and left them on your dock without any water."

"Aw, it didn't hurt 'em!" Homer said. "You're the one who can't take care of periwinkles. They'd die up on a porch."

Suddenly he realized Pam and Rachel had caught

"Let me go!"

up to him. Homer started to run away, but Pam said:

"Give me back that oar! Pete, make him!"

"Get away from me!" Homer shouted defiantly, and gave Pete a push.

Pete shoved him and grabbed the oar. In the tussle it broke apart and fell on the sand.

"Now look what you've done!" Homer screamed and gave Pete a hard punch on the chin which hurt.

Pete punched back, and, in an instant, the boys were fighting hotly. They clinched and rolled over and over. Suddenly Pete landed a hard one on Homer's nose and the boy whimpered:

"I give up! Take your old oar and your silly periwinkles!"

He slunk off down the beach.

"You fixed him good, Pete!" Ricky gloated.

Pete grinned and brushed the sand off his clothes and out of his hair while Pam told the boys about the oar. As soon as they reached home, she found Uncle Russ and told him what Homer had said about getting permission from the mayor before digging for treasure.

"I've never heard of such a thing but I'll check," he said.

Going to the telephone, he called the mayor. In a few minutes, he had his answer and reported to the children.

"For any big operation such as Mr. Ruffly is carrying on," Uncle Russ said, "one does need permission to dig. But for only using shovels in the sand, that's

The whole family set out.

all right. I don't think we'll have any more trouble with Homer and his father.

"Oh, one other thing the mayor told me. Anything that's part of a wreck must be turned over to the museum here."

"Then I'll take the oar over there," Pam promised. "What about other things people find like emeralds?"

"Everything that's not part of a ship is finders keepers," Uncle Russ told her.

"Hurrah!" Ricky shouted. "Let's go dig!"

That afternoon the whole family set out for the special dune, carrying shovels and spades. Suddenly Uncle Russ stopped them and rushed back for his sketching materials.

"Have to make some cartoons of this expedition," he laughed.

First he asked the treasure hunters, all of whom were in bathing suits, to stand in a row by sizes. Mr. Hollister was first with a big shovel. His wife was next carrying a garden spade. Then came Pete, Pam, Holly and Ricky, each with a digging implement. At the end was Sue with a pail and shovel.

"The Happy Hollister Treasure Hunters!" Uncle Russ chuckled as he finished the sketch.

Everyone laughed to see himself drawn with extra large heads and small bodies as cartoons often are. But the faces looked exactly like the artist's relatives.

Uncle Russ continued to make pictures of the diggers as they shoveled and spaded near the dune. The Hollisters found all sorts of unimportant articles like tin cans and broken beach toys, but not one single thing which could have come from the pirate ship they were trying to find.

Holly sighed. "I guess the sea isn't ready to give up its own, just like Scowbanger said."

"Either that," Mr. Hollister replied, "or else that oar was washed here, and the *Mystery's* lying somewhere else."

They gave up but Pete remarked, "We'll find it!"

Early the next morning Rachel came to the house. She held a letter in her hand, which she gave to Mrs. Hollister.

"What does it say?" Sue asked eagerly as her mother pulled out a short note.

Mrs. Hollister read it and smiled. Then she said,

"You children have been invited to eat a sea clam pie at Grandma Alden's."

"Sea clam pie?" Ricky said, scratching his head. "What's that, Rachel?"

The pretty girl gave him a teasing smile and replied, "You'll find out when you eat it. And my grandmother has another surprise, too."

They had been invited for twelve o'clock, so the children swam and played on the beach until eleven. Then they changed into colorful summer clothes and set off with Rachel.

"Is it a hot pie?" Sue wanted to know as they walked along.

"You'll find out," was all Rachel would tell them. When they arrived at Grandma Alden's, what a delicious odor of cooking floated out to them!

Mrs. Alden came in with a clam pie.

"Hm! Yum!" said Ricky. "I guess sea clam pie is good!"

Grandma Alden, her face wreathed in smiles, came out of the kitchen and said that everything was ready. The children took their places at the round dining room table, which had been set with gaily colored plates and napkins. Then Mrs. Alden came in with a large steaming hot pie. She set it on the table and cut wedges for the children.

The Hollisters had not been sure they would like what turned out to be chopped-up clams in sauce put between crusts, but each of them liked the taste and ate two pieces. During the meal the conversation turned to the Mystery, and Pam asked Grandma Alden if she knew anything about the one survivor of the wreck.

"Very little," the woman replied. "He was found by a couple who lived in a half-house, and when he died, they buried him. But a little while afterward both those folks died too. If that survivor told them any secrets, nobody else ever heard them."

Ricky asked what a half-house was and learned it was really a whole house but a small one.

"And now if you've all finished eating," said Grandma Alden after she had served fruit and cookies, "I'll show you a surprise I have for you."

She led them to her workshop in the yard of her home. Inside the shed were all sorts of pottery making materials, and on one side stood a small kiln with a glass door.

"How long does the lighthouse have to cook?"

"Just look in my oven," she invited, "and you'll see a present for the Hollister family. It's baking to make it firm."

The children peered in and saw a lighthouse, larger and more attractive than the one Pete had mended.

"This is made from that fine clay you and Rachel found, Pam," Grandma Alden said. "I want you to use this lamp in place of the one with the crack."

"Oh, that's lovely of you," Pam said and Pete added, "Even Dad's good cement couldn't keep the crack from showing in the other one."

"How long does the lighthouse have to cook?" Sue asked.

Grandma Alden smiled and said two days. Before the Hollisters were ready to leave, Rachel would bring it over to Uncle Russ's house. As the elderly woman began to work on a vase, Pam said:

"We must go now. Thank you ever so much for lunch. The pie was wonderful."

The others thanked her too. Then they said good-by to Grandma Alden and Rachel and walked to the beach.

When they were almost home, Pam stopped short. Putting a hand on Pete's arm, she asked:

"Isn't that Homer Ruffly on our front porch?"

"It sure is," her brother replied. "And there's a man with him. I wonder what they want."

Mr. Hollister was just opening the door for the visitors when the children came up on the porch. Homer introduced the man as his father. He was a short fat man with a large nose, beneath which was a small paintbrush mustache.

"I'd like to speak to you about your boys," he said to Mr. Hollister, as they all sat down in the comfortable chairs.

Pete's and Ricky's hearts began to pound.

What was up?

CHAPTER 13

A Flying Doll

"I UNDERSTAND, Mr. Hollister, that your boys have been picking on Homer and without cause," Mr. Ruffly stated.

"That's right," Homer said.

"Why, Dad!" Pete burst out. "That's not true. We—"

"Just a minute, son," his father waved him into silence. "Let's hear the full accusation."

Mr. Ruffly went on to say that as a boy he himself got into fights but this was out-of-date now. Nice boys just didn't punch one another.

"And you mean Homer doesn't fight?" Mr. Hollister asked.

He could hardly keep from laughing, and his children had broad grins on their faces. Seeing this, Mr. Ruffly replied:

"Of course Homer has to defend himself. But what I really came to talk about was something else. First, suppose we let bygones be bygones. Now I understand that you people are here to hunt for the same pirate ship, the *Mystery*, as I am."

"We're here on a vacation," Mr. Hollister replied.

"The children are enjoying themselves looking for souvenirs. Of course, if they should find a clue to the old ship—"

"That's just the point," Mr. Ruffly interrupted. "They already have found a couple of fine clues. My outfit has located nothing at the spot where they've been working. We're going to move. What do you say we join forces?"

Everyone was startled by the proposal. But instantly the children decided all the fun would be gone if they had to be with Homer Ruffly to hunt for the pirate ship.

"Well, children," Mr. Hollister spoke up. "What do you say?"

Pete jumped to his feet and faced his father. Then he burst out:

"I say *no!*"

"Good for you!" Ricky cried. "I'd rather work by ourselves."

"And I would, too," said Pam.

"And me," Holly added.

"Well, Mr. Ruffly," said Mr. Hollister, "I guess you have your answer."

The treasure hunter was so angry he arose abruptly and said, "Come on, Homer. I've never met such rude, ungrateful people," and stormed off the porch.

A few feet from the house, Homer turned and cried, "You'll be sorry! We'll find the treasure alone, and we won't give you any of it like we were going to!"

"Daddy," said Sue, "are we really rude and under-grates?"

Her father laughed and said he thought it was the Rufflys who were rude. As for being ungrateful, well, maybe the Hollisters had missed a good chance. But working with unpleasant people was a hard way to make money.

"I suggest you all forget the whole thing and go play on the beach."

"Want to see my new kite, Dad?" Pete asked. "It's finished. There's a good wind. I'll try it out."

He went to his room and returned with the new kite. While he was gone, Uncle Russ had come home. He looked in amazement at Pete's invention.

"That's a dandy!" he exclaimed, looking over the intricate work.

"It looks just like a sea gull," Pam remarked.

The kite, about five feet wide, had two wings which were bent just like a gull's. The front of the kite was shaped like a bird's head, and the tail was spread as if it were a beautiful white gull in flight.

"It even has feet!" Sue laughed.

"Let's try it out right away," Ricky said enthusiastically.

They all raced down to the beach. Pete let out a lot of string, and Uncle Russ held the kite aloft some distance away.

"Let 'er go!" Pete shouted, and began to run.

The big, paper sea gull rose gracefully into the

132

air. As the wind caught the kite, it soared higher and higher.

"It's nifty," Ricky praised him. "You ought to win a prize in the contest."

As Pete reeled in his paper sea gull, he noticed that Rachel had joined the group. She as well as Pam complimented him. Then his sister said:

"Remember? Girls are allowed in this contest, aren't they?"

"Sure. Are you thinking of building a kite?"

Pam winked at Rachel and said, "Come on, let's get it now."

"Get what?" Pete wanted to know.

"You'll see in a minute," Pam replied, as she raced off with her friend.

In a few minutes, the girls returned. Between them,

The big paper sea gull rose gracefully.

they were holding a box kite that resembled a big doll.

"Yikes, that's keen!" Ricky cried.

"It sure is," Pete agreed. "It sure ought to win a prize," he remarked. "That is, if it can fly," he added teasingly.

"Of course it can," Pam said. "Let's try it, Rachel."

The box kite rose quickly in the strong breeze and looked even more like a lovely big doll than it did on the ground. As the children watched, they suddenly saw another kite flying not far away. In a moment, its owner appeared over a nearby dune, holding the string attached to it.

Homer Ruffly!

His kite skipped to the right and left, coming very close to the box kite.

"Hey, Homer," Pete shouted. "Don't let the strings cross."

Homer acted as if he did not hear. His kite dipped again, coming even closer to the flying doll.

"Oh, his string has crossed ours!" Pam cried. "I do hope they don't tangle."

"He's doing it on purpose!" Rachel declared, trying to run out of the path of the other kite.

"He's just trying to get even with us," Pete said. Then he shouted again, "Homer! Get your kite out of the way!"

Instead of doing this, the other boy began to jerk at his kite string.

"He's trying to saw your string in two," Pete said to Pam. "That's a mean trick."

"He's trying to saw your string in two!"

All the children shouted at Homer, but he continued to saw the two kite strings together.

"Oh, dear!" Rachel exclaimed. "If our kite string breaks, our lovely doll will be broken, and it took us so long to make it. We never could get another ready for the contest!"

But suddenly something strange happened. Homer's kite leaped higher into the air.

His string had broken instead of Pam's!

"See what happens, smarty?" Ricky shouted, as Homer's kite disappeared out of sight behind the dunes.

Homer spluttered something which the children could not hear, then picked up a stone and threw it toward the box kite. Fortunately, the stone came nowhere near it. Homer turned and ran off in search of his runaway toy.

"I'm glad we're rid of him," Rachel said.

Not long afterwards the sky became cloudy, and the wind grew stronger.

"I think you'd better pull your kite down before the wind snaps it," Pete advised.

The girls carefully brought it down, and they all walked back to the house. Just before suppertime, Ricky and Holly decided to take Zip for a run on the beach. The dog stayed nearby for several minutes, dashing in and out of the water and barking at the waves. Then suddenly he spied another dog some distance away and raced toward him.

"Look! The other dog's digging!" Ricky said. "I wonder what he found."

The strange dog's body was half hidden in a hole not far from the water's edge. But as Zip came up, the other animal jerked himself out and growled. Zip sniffed at the hole. The Airedale snapped at him.

"Say, I'll bet that's Homer's dog!" Ricky cried. "I saw him on the barge when I was getting my periwinkles. His name's Mike."

Holly giggled. "Even their dog's unfriendly." She turned to Zip. "Come on home," she ordered.

But Zip had no intention of leaving. He wanted to find out what was in the hole and began to dig in it.

But immediately Mike nipped his ear. Then a fight started. Both dogs snarled and bit as they tumbled about.

"Stop it! Stop it!" Pam screamed.

But the animals paid no attention. Suddenly Ricky had an idea.

"Let's try to get the dogs in the water, Holly. That'll fix 'em!"

The two children moved in on the fighting animals from the land side. Foot by foot Zip and Mike were shoved toward the water. Then suddenly a big wave rolled in, and the dogs were knocked over.

Before they could resume their fight, Holly had grabbed Zip by his collar and Ricky had Mike's.

"We'd better go home with Zip," said Holly.

"But I want to find out what's in that hole," Ricky objected. "I'll tell you what. You lead Zip home. I'll stay here a little while."

"Okay," Holly agreed. "But don't be long. It's nearly suppertime."

Then a fight started.

When Zip was a safe distance away, Ricky let Mike free. But instead of returning to the hole to dig, the dog ran off toward the ocean.

Left alone, Ricky looked into the opening. He could see something black and rusty buried in the sand. Digging with both hands, the boy finally uncovered enough of the object to recognize it.

"An old anchor!" he told himself.

Scooping away more sand, Ricky suddenly realized that the letter M was staring at him. Then a Y, and finally he uncovered the complete word, MYSTERY!

"Yikes!" the boy shouted. "This is great! I must take this home!"

He kept on working until the whole anchor could be seen. By this time the opening in the sand was so deep that only the top of Ricky's head showed. He climbed out and then reached down to haul up the anchor. It would not budge.

"I'll have to get somebody to help me," the boy decided. He looked around, but the beach was deserted. "I'll go home."

Bursting with his secret, he ran all the way. Out of breath, he rushed in and told his family, who were already at the table, about the wonderful find.

"Let's go right back and get it!" he urged.

But Mrs. Hollister, although she was excited too, thought that they should finish their supper first. But everyone hurried, and, in fifteen minutes, they were on their way.

Ricky led the way, scampering over bits of drift-

The anchor would not budge.

wood and large sea shells along the beach. The boy was so excited and ran so fast that even Pete had trouble keeping up with him.

"Hey, wait a minute, Ricky!" his brother shouted. "That anchor won't fly away!"

The younger boy, some twenty yards ahead, turned and beckoned Pete to hurry.

"This is a real important clue!" he called out. "I don't want anybody to get it before we do!"

Ricky raced ahead and reached the hole first. As he peeked in, a look of complete bewilderment came over his face.

The old anchor was gone!

CHAPTER 14

The Half-House

THE HOLLISTER family stared at the empty hole in the sand for a few seconds. Then Uncle Russ said:

"Ricky, was this one of your jokes?"

"No. Honest. An anchor really was here. I was going to bring it home but I couldn't get it out."

"Look!" said Pete. "There's sort of an outline of a small anchor."

"Yes, there is," his father agreed. "The anchor probably came from one of the small boats on the Mystery. I'm sorry about your disappointment, Ricky. We'll try to track down your anchor."

"I—I was going to give it to the museum 'cause I dug it up," Ricky said, holding back the tears. "But maybe Mike ought to get the credit. He really found it."

"Mike?" Mr. Hollister repeated. "Who's he?"

"A dog. And I think he belongs to Homer." After Ricky told the others about the episode on the beach, he added, "Say, do you suppose Mike brought the Rufflys back here, and they took the anchor?"

His father agreed it sounded very plausible. If Ricky would like to find out, his father would take him to see Homer.

"Only we don't know where he lives," Ricky said.

This was true. Nevertheless, Mr. Hollister thought they could learn this easily enough. First, they would go to the barge. There might be a watchman there who could tell them.

As the other Hollisters started for home, Ricky and his dad went toward the river. Reaching the mouth of it, they found the dock empty. Not only was there no watchman, but Mr. Ruffly's barge and all the equipment were gone! After the Hollisters had recovered from their astonishment, Mr. Hollister said:

"Well, son, it looks as if this is our evening for having things disappear."

"Yes," said Ricky. "Now what are we going to do?"

"Well you decide," his father answered. "We can go home or we can play detective. Which do you want to do?"

Ricky grinned. "Let's find Homer."

Mr. Hollister led the way to town and went straight to the mayor's house. He introduced himself and his son, then had Ricky tell his story to the official.

"This is very unusual," said Mayor Harper. "I haven't given the treasure hunters permission to move to another spot. The Rufflys are staying at the Sea View Hotel. We'll go there and talk to them."

But when the visitors arrived at the hotel, they were told that the Rufflys, their diver and the two other men in the party had checked out.

"Do you know where they went?" Mayor Harper asked the clerk.

"They didn't say. Sorry I can't be of any help."

Mr. Hollister turned to his son. "I guess you're not sorry to see Homer move out, are you, Ricky?" he asked.

"No. Only he took the anchor."

As there seemed to be nothing more they could do, the Hollisters thanked the mayor and said good night. After they reached home and told the family what they had learned, Pete said he was sure Mr. Ruffly had not given up the treasure hunt.

The Rufflys had checked out.

"What do you mean?" Mr. Hollister asked.

"Maybe he let the other men go, and the barge," Pete answered. "But I'm sure Mr. Ruffly and Homer are around here yet."

"Perhaps they'll watch us in the daytime," Pam spoke up, "and then if we find a clue, they'll come at night and dig there."

The speculation might have gone on for some time, but the doorbell rang and interrupted it. A messenger had come with two telegrams—one for Mr. Hollister and the other for Uncle Russ.

"Where's yours from?" Sue asked eagerly when her father finished reading his.

"From Tinker."

"Is he sick or something?" the little girl asked, worried.

"No. It's good news. Only I guess it'll take me home."

Mr. Hollister went on to say that a customer had come into *The Trading Post* to buy a big order of toys. He was a wealthy man who planned to entertain three hundred children at an outing.

"Three hundred!" Holly exclaimed.

"That's certainly a large order," her father said.

"Of course there aren't that many toys in stock at the store. I'll have to return at once to buy more so I can fill the order. Besides the profit I'll make, I'd like to see those children enjoy themselves."

"That's a super order," Pete remarked. Then he asked, "Will we all have to go home?"

143

"They're here!"

"Well—" his father was just beginning to say when Uncle Russ interrupted him.

"The children mustn't go now," he said. "My telegram is from Aunt Marge. She's bringing Teddy and Jean here tomorrow."

"Oh, Dad, please let us stay," Pam begged. "It'll be so much fun to play with our cousins again!"

Uncle Russ said his family was arriving by plane the next morning at nearby Wellsport.

"I suppose," said Mr. Hollister, "that I could fly home by plane, and leave you the car, Elaine. Let's make plans to do that."

A call was made to the airport, and Mr. Hollister was told that he could get a plane for Shoreham at ten-fifteen in the morning.

"My folks come in at ten," said Uncle Russ, "so we can make it in one trip."

The Hollister children rose early, eager for the ride to Wellsport. Their father packed his suitcase and, together with Uncle Russ, they all set off in the station wagon directly after breakfast.

"Sometime let's go on a long plane ride," Ricky remarked as he watched a pilot take off in a small private ship.

"I'll keep that in mind," his father promised, smiling. "And I suppose you'll want to run the plane," he teased.

They drove up to the airfield's offices a few minutes before Aunt Marge's plane was due. The children watched as their Dad got his ticket and had his baggage weighed. Then they heard a droning overhead, and rushed outside to watch a large silvery plane circle the field and finally land. As the door was opened, Holly cried:

"They're here!"

Uncle Russ hurried forward to greet his wife and children, then the Hollisters raced up to their cousins. What a happy reunion with hugs and kisses and exciting chatter!

"You must help us find a treasure," Pete said, putting an arm around Teddy's shoulders.

"And I have an adorable box kite," Pam told Jean. "I've entered it in the contest."

Aunt Marge, slender and pretty, with lovely dark

145

eyes and a happy smile, said she could hardly wait to see Sea Gull Beach.

"And will you make some of your extra special fudge for all of us?" Ricky asked.

"I surely will," she promised.

"Oh, goody!" Sue piped up. "But we have to put Daddy on his plane first."

Everybody laughed, and Mr. Hollister said he was sorry to miss the candy. His plane came in a few minutes later. He kissed his family good-by and climbed the steps to the cabin.

Presently it sped down the runway and soared into the air. The children waved until the plane was out of sight. Then they hurried to the station wagon for the ride back to Sea Gull Beach.

They waved until the plane was out of sight.

Uncle Russ took a back road to avoid traffic, and they all became very interested in the countryside through which he drove. From the condition of the land and the tumble-down houses it was apparent that no one had lived in some of the places for a long time.

"I've heard fishermen used to stay here when there was a good inlet," Uncle Russ said. "It's all filled in with sand now."

As he turned into a road that was not far from the shore front, Pam called out, "See that little house over there! Is that what you call a half-house?"

"I think it is," Uncle Russ replied. "And I'd like to stop and make a sketch of it."

He drove into the weedy, hardly visible lane and parked. Pulling a pad and pencil from a pocket of his sport coat, he began to draw.

Meanwhile, the children had jumped out of the station wagon. Pam told her cousins about Grandma Alden and her story that the one survivor of the *Mystery* had been found by a couple who lived in a half-house.

"It could even be this one!" she said excitedly. "Let's look around."

"Don't forget it was a hundred years ago that the wreck happened," Pete reminded his sister. "What could you find here now?"

Just then they saw a man coming across a field. When he reached them, the farmer said he had seen the Hollister car stop and wondered if he could give

"Is it all right to look around?"

them any information. This was part of his property.

"My uncle wanted to draw a picture of the half-house," Pam answered politely. "Can you tell us why it's called that?"

The question pleased the farmer very much. Sitting down on an old tree stump, he explained that in colonial days newly married couples who had little money built only a small house for themselves.

"It usually was big enough for a few years," he said, smiling at the children. "Then, as their family grew, they would add a room here and a room there until they had a big house."

"Then I guess the people who built this place never had a family," Pam remarked.

"That's right," the farmer agreed. "The old couple

148

lived all their lives without any children and their little home remained a half-house. Nobody has lived in it since, I understand."

"Is it all right to look around?" Pam asked.

She was tempted to tell the man why but decided not to.

The farmer said they might investigate, but he warned them that the place was very rickety. The children should be careful not to get hurt. When Mrs. Hollister heard this, she went with them.

The man opened a creaking front door, and they went inside. How musty the old place was! And the rooms were so tiny, the visitors filled them up!

It did not take long to examine the living room and kitchen on the first floor and the one bedroom on

"Oh, it's spooky down here!"

the second. Then Pete and Ricky led the way into the most mysterious part of the house—a little round cellar at the foot of a flight of very steep steps.

"Oh, it's spooky down here," Ricky said, "and dark, too."

"Let's get the flashlight from the car," Pete suggested.

Holly ran for it and gave it to Pete. Then, while Mrs. Hollister and the girls waited, the three boys went all the way down. The cellar walls were lined with brick but the floor was just plain earth.

"Hold the light on the steps," Pam called. "Jean and I are coming down."

Teddy held the light while Ricky and Pete started to poke around. Suddenly the flashlight shone on a piece of oblong marble imbedded in the dirt.

"I wonder what this is," Ricky said.

Pete picked up a sharp stick and pried around the slab. Then he and Teddy lifted it up for everyone to see.

"Roaring rockets!" Pete exclaimed. "It's an old tombstone!"

On the reverse side was an inscription, but the children could not read it because the stone was covered with dirt.

"Let's take it outside and look at it," Pam suggested.

The slab was not very heavy, and Pete and Teddy easily carried it to the yard. When the farmer saw it, he chuckled.

"Read what it says," Holly begged.

"I saw that thing down there years ago," he said. "But I never dreamed it was an old tombstone. Let's see what it says."

Pam already was busy scraping the dirt off the inscription with a stick.

"Read what it says," Holly begged her.

Pam looked at it for a moment, puzzled. "It's not like regular tombstones," she told them all. "It says:

A Mystery Man
Though a Pirate he be
Loved his Ship and the Stormy Sea
All was lost on the Bounding Main
Where the Frog Rock looks Across to Spain."

CHAPTER 15

An Exciting Afternoon

"IT's THE clue we need!" Pete shouted. "All we have to do is find the Frog Rock and dig up the treasure!"

"Mother, what *is* Pete talking about?" Sue asked, tugging at her mother's arm.

"And I'd like to know, too," the farmer spoke up.

Mrs. Hollister briefly told him the story they had heard about the lone survivor of the *Mystery*, then explained to Sue that Spain was right across the ocean from Sea Gull Beach.

"I suppose," she smiled, "that the rock which looks like a frog is pointed in that direction. The *Mystery* must have been wrecked there."

Turning to the farmer, she asked, "Do you know where the Frog Rock is?"

"Never heard of it," he answered.

"But we're going to find the rock!" Ricky declared. "Let's go!"

Uncle Russ copied the inscription from the tombstone on his pad. Then the boys replaced the old slab in the basement.

Mrs. Hollister thanked the farmer for letting them look around, then the visitors started for Sea Gull

"To think you found the clue!"

Beach. Teddy and Jean were terribly excited to have arrived in the middle of the detective case that their cousins were solving.

"Why don't we ask Grandma Alden about Frog Rock?" Pete proposed when they reached the house.

He and Teddy carried the suitcases inside. Then he and Pam and their cousins hurried to the elderly woman's home. She was glad to see them again and so was Rachel, whom Pete and Pam introduced to their cousins.

Upon hearing the story of the inscription, Grandma Alden threw up her hands and said, "My goodness! People have been looking for that clue for more than fifty years. And to think you Hollister children came all the way from Shoreham to find it!"

153

When Pam asked her about the Frog Rock, a far-away look came into the elderly woman's eyes.

"Yes, I remember the Frog Rock," she said. "But I'm a little hazy about where it is. It seems to me something happened to it. Scowbanger might know."

"Let's go ask him," Pete suggested eagerly.

"Wait, children. Maybe you won't have to go to his shack to find him. He comes into town to shop about this time of day," Grandma Alden told them. "Rachel, suppose you run down to the market and look for him?"

Her granddaughter hurried off and returned with Scowbanger about fifteen minutes later.

"What's all this about the old Frog Rock?" the old man asked with a broad smile. "That brings back memories of the days before our big storm."

Scowbanger went on to say that the rock, which looked much like a frog's head, had stood on the edge of a high dune for many years. Then, during a violent storm, the earth beneath it had been undermined, and the rock had tumbled into the sea.

"Do you know where?" Pam asked.

Scowbanger squinted his left eye. "Well, just about." And then he added, "You might be able to find it at low tide."

"The tide will be out tomorrow morning at nine," Grandma Alden said, her eyes twinkling.

The children looked eagerly at Scowbanger, who slapped his knee and exclaimed, "Then we'll hunt for the Frog Rock tomorrow morning at nine!"

He left them to continue his marketing. As the Hollister children were about to go, Grandma Alden asked them if they wouldn't like to accompany Rachel to a food sale for the benefit of the local school.

"The PTA is raising money for pictures," she said. "The walls are very bare."

"We'd love to go," Pam answered for all of them. Then smiling she added, "Grandma Alden, did you donate a sea clam pie?"

"Yes I did."

"Then I'm going to buy it so Jean and Teddy can taste how good it is."

The elderly woman's eyes lighted up at the compliment.

"And I'm going to do something for the school,"

"Then we'll hunt for the Frog Rock!"

Teddy announced. "I'll ask Dad for a picture." When Grandma Alden looked startled, he said, "Oh I don't mean a cartoon—one of his regular pictures."

"Why that's splendid," she said.

The Hollisters skipped off but were back soon after lunch. Ricky and Holly were with them. They hurried with Rachel to the center of town.

What a hustle and bustle there was on the village green where the sale was being held! Several colorful booths had been set up. Besides the food which was on sale there were games for children.

"Oh, I want to get a prize out of the fish pond!" Holly said, dashing off to try her luck.

"And I want to put out the lights on those candles with a squirt gun!" Ricky cried, running over to play the game.

Teddy and Pete went off to find the president of the PTA and give her the lovely landscape which Uncle Russ had donated to the school.

"I'd better get your grandmother's pie, Rachel, before they sell it to someone else," Pam remarked. "Come on, girls."

They went to the pie table, and she bought it. Then they moved to the cake booth where Holly purchased a dozen doughnuts. As Rachel was asking the price of a three-layer chocolate cake, Pam cried out:

"Look! There's Homer Ruffly!"

"Really?" Holly asked. Then she added with a sigh, "How are we going to keep the Frog Rock a secret with him around?"

Homer aimed the water at Ricky.

"We'll certainly have to be careful," Pam said. "Oh, girls, see what he's doing!"

With this, Pam started to run. The others could see why. Homer was standing behind a booth, a squirt gun in his hand. He was aiming a stream of water straight at Ricky!

On the first try it did not quite reach. But the second shot hit the boy in one ear.

"Hey! Ouch! What?" Ricky howled, clapping his hand to his head.

Homer had dodged behind the booth so Ricky could not see where the water had come from. In a moment Homer appeared on the other side of the booth and aimed the water pistol. But before he could pull the trigger, Pam grabbed his arm. It swung around and the water went all over his face.

"Good for you, Pam!" Ricky cried, realizing it was Homer who had used the squirt gun on him.

For good measure, he turned his own water pistol on Homer, who cried out that he was getting soaked.

"Better stop," Pam advised her brother, seeing the woman who ran the candle game coming toward the boys.

He handed her the toy gun and then said to Homer, "We thought you'd gone home. What did you do with the anchor?"

"Why we took it to—" Suddenly Homer stopped. He remembered he was telling something he was not supposed to. "What anchor are you talking about? I don't know anything about an anchor."

Ricky and the girls stared at Homer. Pam thought maybe she could find out if he knew about the anchor by trying something else.

"Where are you staying?" she asked.

"Try and find out," Homer said rudely. Then he added, "We're going to find the treasure any minute now. And it's in a secret place."

Homer ran off. The girls and Ricky looked at one another in dismay. But when Pete came up with Teddy and heard the story, he said he was sure Homer was only fooling about finding the treasure.

"Let's forget that meanie and buy some candy," Ricky urged.

He led the way toward a blue and yellow bunting booth and eyed the homemade sweets hungrily. He bought two coconut molasses balls and the others took taffy and caramels.

"We can't carry any more," Pam laughed. "We'd better go home!"

The Hollisters said good-by to Rachel and went to their own house. They found Sue giggling over a cartoon strip which Uncle Russ had just finished.

It showed a kite flying contest. A little boy with an enormous kite was being carried up into the air by it.

"Of course, this couldn't happen," Uncle Russ said with a grin, "but it would be a thrill, wouldn't it?"

"I'd like to take a ride like that," Ricky exclaimed, looking at the pictures. "Way up high."

"Maybe you can," the cartoonist said.

They eyed the homemade sweets hungrily.

"What do you mean, Uncle Russ?"

The man put his arm around Ricky's shoulder. "I wasn't going to tell you until later," he said, "but I have a big surprise coming for all of you at seven o'clock tonight."

Although all the children begged him to tell them what the surprise was, Uncle Russ refused.

Jean said, "Oh, please, Daddy! Don't keep us in suspense. Is it a ride in a motorboat?"

When Uncle Russ said no, Ricky asked, "Are you going to build us a giant kite that can pull us into the air?"

"Well, you're getting warm," their uncle replied with a chuckle. "But I'm afraid you'll have to wait and see."

After supper, the children kept watching the clock. As the hands approached seven, Uncle Russ said:

"All of you come down to the beach with me."

Mystified, the children followed him out on the sand. Waiting expectantly, they saw him look at his watch several times.

Suddenly he smiled and looked up. Overhead they heard a noise which sounded like a whole pack of motorcycles.

"It's a helicopter!" Teddy exclaimed.

"Is this your surprise?" Pam asked, her voice full of excitement.

Uncle Russ nodded. "This is it."

The helicopter came lower and lower, its blades fanning the air so fast that they were as transparent

The helicopter came lower and lower.

as a dragonfly's wings. It settled down onto the beach about twenty feet from where the Hollisters were standing.

The cabin door opened and the pilot stepped down.

"I'm here to pick up your sketches, Mr. Hollister," he said to Uncle Russ.

"Nice work, Sky," Uncle Russ said, walking over and shaking hands with the man.

Then he introduced him to the Hollister children. The man's name was John Larkin, but all his friends called him Sky. Uncle Russ sent Teddy back to the house to pick up the package of sketches which lay on a table. When the boy returned with them, Uncle Russ said:

"How would all you children like to go for a ride in the copter? Maybe you'll see the Frog Rock."

CHAPTER 16

"Thar She Blows!"

"YIKES!" Ricky exclaimed. "A ride in a copter!"

Uncle Russ suggested that Sue, Jean, Holly and Pam be the first to go up with Sky Larkin. The girls scrambled into the helicopter, and the pilot shut the door.

The big rotors whirred, lifting them into the air. As they went along the shore front, Pam and Jean looked hard for a rock resembling a frog but could not see one. Fifteen minutes later they were back. When they landed, the four girls jumped down to the sand.

"Oh, it was simply wonderful!" Pam cried in delight. "You boys will just love it!"

Pete, Ricky, Teddy and Uncle Russ stepped into the helicopter. When it rose into the air, Sky Larkin asked, "Would you like to take a spin out over the ocean?"

"Oh, yes," the boys answered together.

From that height, the waves looked very green, and the whitecaps had lacy edges. Suddenly Pete pointed out across the water.

"Is that a submarine out there?"

Something dark lay on the surface of the sea. Then

all at once a long plume of white mist spouted up from the object.

"It's a whale!" Pete shouted.

"You're right," Sky agreed. "Would you like to get a closer look at him?"

"Oh, yes."

Sky guided the helicopter straight toward the whale, at the same time dropping closer to the water.

"I hope this noise doesn't scare him away," Teddy said, as they approached the long, black whale.

But the big mammal did not move. Soon they were directly over him. Sky said:

"Pete, come up here if you want a better look."

The boy came forward and leaned out the pilot's window. As he peered down at the gigantic creature, the pilot called out:

"Thar she blows!"

"Thar she blows!"

Another plume of spray suddenly spouted up from the head of the whale directly at the helicopter. Before Pete could duck back in, the strong stream of salt water hit him full force!

"Ugh!" Pete cried, pulling his head back into the helicopter.

Though he was a sorry sight, the boy was not harmed, and the others had to laugh. They offered handkerchiefs and scarfs for him to wipe his head and arms, but Pete declared that all he wanted right now was a good bath in fresh water.

"That wasn't so bad as being in the whale's tummy like Jonah," Teddy teased him.

"You ought to be proud," Ricky grinned. "I'll bet you're the only boy a whale ever spouted at."

"Well, I'll trade places with you," Pete said.

But the whale had dived and gone off. Sky took the helicopter back to the beach. His passengers climbed out, and he took off. As the Hollisters went back to the house, Uncle Russ said to the children:

"Tomorrow's the big day, isn't it? I expect you to locate the pirates' treasure."

"Oh, wouldn't it be wonderful?" Pam cried.

Scowbanger kept his appointment. Next morning he drove Jenny Jump up in front of the Hollister house, and all the children, as well as Zip, hopped in. The old man drove them several miles down the beach, then stopped his buggy.

"All out here!" he said. "The old Frog Rock is somewhere in this vicinity."

It was ebb tide and the shore seemed to stretch far out into the ocean. Scowbanger pointed to several large, black rocks strewn along the beach near the water's edge.

"I think one of these might be the Frog Rock you're looking for," he said.

All the children, who were in bathing suits, splashed through the shallow water out to the round, slippery rocks. They examined them one after another. But none looked anything like a frog's head.

"Well," Scowbanger said, squinting his eyes and peering along the shore, "maybe my old memory's failing me. I thought sure this was the place where 'the Frog Rock looked across to Spain.' "

The children in their search had been too busy to pay attention to Zip. He had been teasing a baby crab, but now the dog bounded off down the beach.

Suddenly the collie began to bark. When the children turned to look at him, Zip was far down the shore. His front paws were resting on a large rock and he was staring at a sea gull perched on top of it.

"Let's go down there," Ricky said eagerly. "Maybe that's the Frog Rock."

They ran along the sand, finally coming to the place where their pet was. The sea gull had flown away, and the dog was sniffing in the sand.

Hopefully the children walked around the rock to see what it looked like.

"It looks just like a frog's head."

"I don't think this is it, do you?" Pam asked.

Pete viewed the rock from another angle. Then suddenly he said excitedly:

"Come here!"

The others ran to his side, where they caught a good profile view of the rock.

"It looks just like a frog's head!" Ricky shouted.

"We've found it! We've found it!" Holly screamed jubilantly.

By this time Scowbanger had caught up to the children in the beach buggy. Pete showed him the likeness of a frog's head, and he grinned happily.

"Congratulations to you! The Hollisters have found the place where the *Mystery* went down!"

"Zip found it," Sue spoke up staunchly.

"Now what'll we do?" Jean asked. "The ship's probably under water."

They held a little parley. Teddy thought maybe they should notify the town authorities, but the others talked him out of this.

"Let's try to find it ourselves," Pete urged.

"Let's dig right now," Ricky cried excitedly, as he looked around for something to dig with.

Scowbanger said they would need strong tools to dig in the sand and they would have to hurry too if they expected to do much before the tide came in. And besides, a storm was brewing. The beachcomber had an idea.

"How about Ricky and me standin' guard here with the girls while you, Pete, and Teddy take the beach buggy and fetch some shovels from your house?"

"Swell," said Pete enthusiastically. He grinned. "Is Jenny Jump fixed so she'll stop when I want her to?"

"Yes indeed. I fixed her so she won't play any more tricks."

The boys hopped in, and Pete drove away quickly. As they reached the area where the bathers were, he had to slow down and skirt them carefully.

"With this traffic jam, the tide'll start coming in before we get back," Pete grumbled.

But finally they reached their house and stopped. The boys rushed in to tell their families the exciting news and the grownups were astounded.

"You've really found the site of the missing pirate ship, *Mystery!*" Uncle Russ exclaimed. "Wonderful!"

"We'll all go back with you," Aunt Marge said.

The shovels and spades and even a rusty pick were collected. Pete ran outside ahead of the others to start the car.

At the wheel sat Homer Ruffly!

"Hey, get out of there!" Pete shouted.

"I will not!" Homer said. "I guess I can run this as much as you!"

But Homer saw fire in Pete's eye. He did not want to be beaten in another fight. A sly scheme came to him. Quickly pulling the car key out of the ignition, he put it into his pocket. Then he jumped and started to run.

"Try and get the old buggy started!" he shouted gleefully.

Pete instantly knew what Homer had done and

At the wheel sat Homer Ruffly!

gave chase. The trickster had a good head start, and though Pete ran as fast as he could, he was not able to catch Homer.

"But he won't get away with this!" Pete determined.

On and on they went. Homer was headed for the river. Reaching it, he jumped into a motorboat, untied it and pushed the starter button. The motor did not catch at once. Homer fumed. Pete was getting closer.

Then suddenly the engine roared into life. Just as Homer steered from the dock, Pete reached it. With a flying leap he landed in the motorboat.

"Give me that key, Homer!" he shouted.

Homer paid no attention. By this time the boat was racing along at a good clip. As Pete moved up front to Homer, it sped out of the channel into the ocean.

"Give me that key and turn around!" Pete demanded.

"Nothing doing," Homer replied. "I'll throw the key overboard before I'll give it to you!"

Pete tried to grab the steering wheel, but the other boy gave him a shove. By this time they were out beyond the breakers. Still Homer did not turn.

"Where are you going?" Pete said, trying to yank the wheel about.

Suddenly a look of fright came over Homer's face. "This wheel—it's stuck! I can't turn back!" he cried in alarm.

CHAPTER 17

The Hurricane

THE MOTORBOAT continued to speed toward the horizon as Homer tugged at the wheel.

"Turn off the motor!" Pete shouted above the whistling wind.

Homer seemed too frightened. Pete leaned over and clicked off the switch. The boat slowed but did not stop.

"Here comes someone," Pete cried.

A man in a low-slung powerboat passed them at a little distance. Pete thought he was Uncle Russ's next door neighbor. The boy rose and waved his arms, shouting for help. The man evidently could not hear him and merely thought the boy was being friendly. He waved back and continued on toward shore.

The current continued to carry the motorboat out into the ocean. By this time the beach was so far distant that Pete could not distinguish familiar landmarks. If help did not come quickly, they might be lost at sea!

Homer began to cry. "Oh, why did I take this old thing out?" he whimpered. Putting his hand into his pocket, he pulled out the key to Scowbanger's beach buggy and handed it to Pete.

"Maybe if you take this, I—I'll be forgiven and we'll be rescued."

Pete was completely disgusted with Homer, but he had little time to think about it. He kept standing, hoping that by some miracle the boys would be seen.

"How will we ever get back?" Homer wailed. "Oh, if we only had oars along, we could row back."

"But we haven't," said Pete tersely.

After the boys had floated around for half an hour, the sky began to grow dark.

"An awful storm's coming up!" Homer burst out, glancing up at the ominous black clouds that were rolling close to the surface of the sea.

A few minutes later a strong wind whipped the waves into frothy whitecaps and a few drops of rain fell on the boys' faces. The boat began to pitch and toss.

"We'll overturn and drown!" Homer wailed.

Pete told him to keep up his courage. "If we lie down in the bottom of the boat, we may be able to ride this storm out," he said.

The boys did this, covering themselves with a tarpaulin to keep off the rain, which now came pelting down in sweeping white sheets. As the wind grew more violent, the waves became higher and the boat pitched up and down at a frightening angle. Lightning flashed and thunder boomed over the churning sea.

171

The boat pitched at a frightening angle.

All at once Pete thought he heard the motor of another boat. Lifting his head up from under the tarpaulin, he listened intently. He was not mistaken! As the sound grew closer, the boy raised himself on his knees and peered about. Then he scrambled up, waving his arms wildly.

"Homer, a boat! It's come to rescue us!"

The other boy stood up in time to see a large launch making its way toward them. It was a white boat, and on the prow were the words *Coast Guard*.

Four men were in the boat. Pete at first could not distinguish who they were. But when the craft pulled alongside, he noticed that one of the men in an oilskin slicker was Uncle Russ. The three others were Coast Guardsmen.

"Thank goodness we found you!" Uncle Russ said. "If it hadn't been for my neighbor, we wouldn't have known where you were."

The men held the two boats together, and the boys scrambled into the large launch. Then one of the seamen tied Homer's motorboat onto the back of the launch, and they headed for the shore.

"Now, suppose you two fellows tell us how you happened to be out here," Uncle Russ urged.

Pete disliked being a tattletale so he did not speak up at once. Homer, evidently frightened at what he had done, told the story.

"I was only fooling," he concluded. "And I gave Pete the key, and I was going right back, but I couldn't." He began to whimper again. "My—my father's going to punish me for breaking his boat."

The Hollisters hoped that Homer had learned his lesson, but nevertheless Pete said, "The rudder's only

"Homer, a boat! It's come to rescue us!"

jammed. It can be fixed easily." Then he turned to the Coast Guardsmen. After thanking them, he said, "If we had drifted around for days, I might have missed the kite flying contest day after tomorrow."

One of the men smiled. "I hear it's going to be the biggest contest yet."

When the launch arrived at the Coast Guard dock, the rest of the Hollister family, Scowbanger and Mr. Ruffly were there to meet them. Mrs. Hollister hugged Pete, but Mr. Ruffly merely grabbed Homer by the arm and shook him.

"You'll be punished for taking the boat as soon as I get it into a dock," he said angrily.

Pete gave Scowbanger the key, and he thanked the boy with a clap on the shoulder. He said they would continue the search the next day, then the old man hurried off. The Hollisters went home, and Pete changed into dry clothing. By suppertime the storm had grown even fiercer. The newscast said it was a hurricane, but that it should pass out to sea during the night. The announcer warned that nobody should go out on the beach until the gale was over.

A letter had come for Pete and he opened it eagerly. It was from Dave Mead who wrote that Joey admitted knowing what had happened to Mr. Sparr's compass. He had seen Zip bury it in the Hollister garden, but had not let on, just for spite. Joey had shown Dave the spot. He had dug up the compass and returned it to the retired sailor.

"Crickets!" exclaimed Pete, and read the whole

Their shovels began to fly.

letter to the others. "Now I can keep the compass I bought to give to Mr. Sparr."

"Zip's mischief turned out okay after all," declared Pam gaily.

Before going to bed, Pete worked on his sea gull kite, painting eyes and a beak on the bird's head. Pam and Holly busied themselves with the doll box kite. When they finished, Pam said:

"Look at this, Pete. I've put the doll's head on a swivel so that it will rock back and forth in the wind."

"Swell. The kite flying judges should like that!"

The children went to sleep, listening to the howling winds. But when they awoke the next morning, the storm had ended and the sun was shining.

"Now we can dig for the pirate treasure," Pete said as they finished breakfast.

The children could hardly wait to pick up the shovels and spades and hurry off down the beach to meet Scowbanger. When they reached the Frog Rock, the beachcomber had not yet arrived.

"How different everything looks here!" Pam remarked as she glanced around the beach.

A hill of sand which had been standing there the day before, now had moved far down the beach. Part of a big dune had washed away, leaving great chunks of clay lying along the edge of the water.

"Where'll we start digging?" Ricky asked.

"Let's start at this low spot," Pete said, pointing out a large area where the wind had already helped to dig a big hole some distance back from the water.

Their shovels began to fly and the hole in the sand grew deeper. Suddenly Ricky's spade hit something. He picked it up. Two old coins!

"Look what I've found!" he shouted.

The others ran to his side and Pete examined the dull brown-colored coins.

"They have Spanish words on them!" he said excitedly. "We must be near the pirate treasure!"

Ricky's find spurred the children to dig even faster. The hole became deeper. All at once Pam's shovel struck something solid. She dropped to her knees and scooped away the sand with her hands.

"There's something wooden buried here!" she called out.

All of the children came to help her clear away the wet sand. More and more of the wood began to show.

It proved to be a plank, and it was connected to another and then another. Finally Pete stood erect, a startled expression coming over his face.

"You know what this is?" he shouted. "It's the deck of a ship!"

"We've found the *Mystery!*" Holly shrieked.

Could it be true? Had they found the wreckage of the pirate ship, which had been lost for a hundred years?

"We still have to prove that this *is* the *Mystery*," Pete reminded the others.

The children dug so fast there was a great shower of flying sand. The larger the hole became the more the deck was revealed. Finally they uncovered the prow of the boat. There, in big copper letters, was its name.

The *Mystery!*

"This is it all right!" Pam cried happily, and all the children whooped and danced.

Suddenly they saw a group of men trudging along the beach. A boy was with them.

"Mr. Ruffly—and Homer!" Ricky cried.

When the men saw the pirate ship, they stared in amazement. Then Mr. Ruffly said:

"So you kids found it!" He laughed loudly. "That's fine. Come on, we'll go down into the hold and get that treasure we've been looking for!"

CHAPTER 18

A Great Victory

"THE pirate ship's not your property, Mr. Ruffly," Pete said stoutly.

"We don't care," Homer's father said defiantly. "We're going to find the treasure in the *Mystery*."

At this moment there was a great chugging, and the beachcomber roared up in his beach buggy.

"Scowbanger!" Pam cried. "We found the *Mystery*, but Mr. Ruffly's going to take the treasure!"

Scowbanger strode over and met the man face to face. "If you touch this ship," he said, "you'll get into real trouble! I'd advise you to leave!"

"We got permission from the mayor to salvage the pirate ship," Mr. Ruffly said.

"So have some other folks," the old man told him. "And included among them are these children. Now get out before I go for the police!"

The treasure hunters looked at one another. Then they began to whisper among themselves. Finally, Mr. Ruffly turned toward Scowbanger, shaking his fist.

"We'll leave now, but we'll be back! I'm going straight to Mayor Harper!"

178

The children were worried. Suppose they had to give up looking for the treasure everyone thought was on board the *Mystery*. Holly mentioned it to Scowbanger.

"Now you stop worrying," he said. "The mayor's not going to let anybody take it away from you. The Rufflys won't be back."

They weren't. As a matter of fact the Hollisters never saw them again. But plenty of other people came. The children's mother, Aunt Marge and Uncle Russ had hurried to Frog Rock to see how the children were making out.

"Why this is amazing!" Mrs. Hollister said, and the others joined in praising them.

Meanwhile Scowbanger had hurried to town and

"I'm going straight to Mayor Harper!"

brought the mayor and the other councilmen back with him.

"I say the Hollisters are the rightful ones to dig for any treasure on this ship," he said.

The men talked a few minutes, then Mayor Harper announced, "We agree. Anything that is not part of the ship itself belongs to the treasure hunters. Of course," he laughed, "Sea Gull Beach wouldn't mind receiving part of it."

"And we'll give it to you!" Pete spoke up.

By this time, word had spread around town that the old pirate ship had been found. It seemed as if every local resident and summer visitor came to look on. The Fraser boys and Rachel appeared.

"We boys would like to help you dig out the *Mystery*," Tom offered.

"We brought our shovels," Tim added with a grin.

With so many willing hands, the broken mast was soon uncovered. Though it was worn and rotting, Ricky begged to have it put in place. The old hole in which it had stood was cleaned out, and the mast was hoisted upright.

"Now I can be a pirate!" Ricky exclaimed, dashing up and down and duelling with an imaginary enemy.

Soon part of the interior was cleaned out. A few minutes later Holly found a small box. When she opened it, mixed in with the sand that had seeped through were gems of all kinds.

"A jewel box!" she cried as the others looked. "Mother, what'll we do with this?"

Mrs. Hollister smiled. "We'll keep whatever Mayor Harper thinks would be a just reward to you children for finding the old wreck. The rest will go to the town."

"Thank you! Thank you!" the mayor said and the councilmen nodded. "Suppose we put the jewels in a safe place and have them appraised. Then we'll send you a check for your share."

What a shout went up from the onlookers!

"The wonderful Happy Hollisters!" cried Rachel who had just come up.

Visitors passed by the pirate ship all afternoon. The digging went on but nothing more was found but a few coins. As the searchers gave up, Scowbanger smiled.

"The rest of the pirate treasure must have been scattered up and down the coast. It's still here for me to find!"

What a happy excited group of children went to bed that night. And the kite flying contest was still to come!

The morning of the seventeenth dawned bright and cheerful with a breeze just right for flying kites. A committee of judges arrived at the beach at noon, and registered each of the contestants. There were nearly a hundred boys and girls. One by one their beautiful kites took the air.

Some went up very high. Others became tangled. Several strings broke and the kites were lost.

Pete's sea gull kite flew beautifully. Pam's and

The judges made notes on slips of paper.

Rachel's doll box kite hovered high in the skies, the doll's head bobbing back and forth.

As the kites wheeled about in the sky, the judges made notes on little slips of paper. Then a man mounted a platform. Holding a microphone in his hand, he said:

"We have selected the three winners of the contest. It was hard because the kites are better and more original than ever before."

Everybody became quiet as the announcer went on, "In the girls' division, the winning kite is the doll box kite entered by Pam Hollister and Rachel Snow."

There was much clapping and cheering. The announcer raised his hand for silence and continued:

"The prize for the largest and finest kite goes to Tom Fraser."

"That's swell," said Pete who was standing next to him.

"And the award for the most unusual kite in the meet goes to—Pete Hollister!"

What cheering and clapping greeted the announcements!

"And now," the man said, "I have a surprise for all of you children. There will be a masquerade party in the basement of the town hall tonight. Prizes will be awarded at that time."

The contestants scattered to their homes to make plans for the big party. That evening they thronged to the town hall in all kinds of costumes. Pam recognized Rachel, who was dressed in a quaint colonial outfit with a pretty pink hoop skirt. The Fraser boys came dressed as three clowns.

But the biggest surprise of all was the Hollister cousins. They were dressed as pirates, with patches over one eye and skulls and crossbones on their black hats. The children played games and ate ice cream and cake.

When the party was at its height, one of the kite contest judges announced that prizes would be awarded.

Pam received a huge rubber seahorse, almost as big as a real horse. It would carry three children.

Tom Fraser was given an aquaplane board, and Pete Hollister received a collapsible rubber boat which could hold two persons.

The children thanked the judge for their prizes, and

after the clapping had died down, the man held up his hands for silence.

"And now I have a special surprise for you," he said. "The town council has decided to leave the pirate ship right where the Hollisters found it. The *Mystery* will be the greatest exhibit at Sea Gull Beach, and any child visiting this place will be allowed to play pirate on it as much as he wishes."

"Three cheers for the Hollisters!" Terry Fraser shouted.

And everybody joined in.

"Hurray! Hurray! Hurray!"